Costa Rica

Costa Rica

Marion Morrison

*Enchantment of the World
Second Series*

Children's Press®

A Division of Grolier Publishing

NEW YORK   LONDON   HONG KONG   SYDNEY
DANBURY, CONNECTICUT

Consultant: George I. Blanskten, Professor Emeritus, Northwestern University

Please note: All statistics are as up-to-date as possible at the time of publication.

Visit Children's Press on the Internet: http://publishing.grolier.com

Book production by Editorial Directions, Inc.
Book design by Ox+Company, Inc.

Library of Congress Cataloging-in-Publication Data

Morrison, Marion.
        Costa Rica / by Marion Morrison.
        p. cm. — (Enchantment of the world. Second series)
        Includes bibliographical references (p.   ) and index.
Summary: Describes the geography, history, culture, religion, and people of the small
        Central American nation of Costa Rica.
        ISBN 0-516-20469-6
        1. Costa Rica—Juvenile literature. [1. Costa Rica] I. Title. II. Series
        F1543.2M67 1998
        972.86—dc21   97-40665
                                                            CIP
                                                            AC

Acknowledgments

The author wishes to thank her many Costa Rican friends for all of their assistance during the research and writing of this book, as well as the Costa Rican embassy in London.

Contents

Cover photo:
Gathering rain clouds

Meseta Central

Scarlet macaw

Welcome to Costa Rica

Christopher Columbus reached Costa Rica in late September 1502. With a flotilla of four small ships, the great navigator had battled against storms along the coast of Central America believing he had reached Asia. He was forced to take shelter near present-day Puerto Limón on the Caribbean coast, where he found a village called Cariai.

H IS ENCOUNTER WITH THE LOCAL PEOPLE IS DESCRIBED vividly: "The people gathered, many of them with bows and arrows and others with spears of palm wood. The men kept their hair long in plaits wound around their heads, and the women's hair was short."

The Native Americans Columbus met wore golden ornaments, and the farther he sailed along the coast, the more gold the people seemed to have. The land was named *Costa Rica*, meaning "rich coast" in Spanish, but the Europeans' dream was short-lived. Most of the gold they had seen came from other parts of Central America. There was no gold near the coast.

Although the lack of minerals was a setback, the Spaniards discovered the land was good for farming. Until the second half of the nineteenth century, when coffee and bananas were first grown in Costa Rica, the people were extremely poor. However, they worked together to survive, and more than that, their closeness to the

Opposite: **The dense forest of Braulio Carrillo National Park**

Christopher Columbus and his crew look for land.

COSTA RICA

- Cities of over 10,000 people
- Smaller cities and towns

| 0 | 400 miles |
| 0 | 600 kilometers |

Managua

NICARAGUA

Lago de Nicaragua

CARIBBEAN SEA

Isla Bolaños

Guanacaste

Península de Santa Elena

Liberia

CORD. DE GUANACASTE

Alajuela

San Juan

Heredia

COSTA RICA

Limón

Punta Blanca

Tilarán

Santa Cruz

Nicoya

San Ramón

Grecia

Moín

Puerto Limón

Turrialba

Cartago

San José

Paraíso

Chirripó Grande
12,530 ft. (3,819 m)

Península de Nicoya

Golfo de Nicoya

San José

Rivas

CORDILLERA DE TALAMANCA

Bahía de Coronado

Ujarrás

Puntarenas

PACIFIC OCEAN

Isla de Caño

Goltito

PANAMA

Santa Domingo

Golfo Dulce

Península de Osa

Punta Burica

COSTA RICA

Isla del Coco (Costa Rica)

Geopolitical map of Costa Rica

land built up over the centuries. This unity, combined with their isolation from other countries, gave the Costa Ricans a stability and tranquillity not shared by their neighbors. While other countries in the region squabbled over minerals, boundaries, and power, the people of Costa Rica developed a strong, well-coordinated society.

Almost all Costa Ricans are descended from European settlers, mainly Spaniards, and over the last 500 years, they have built a cultural heritage they treasure. As early as 1869, their constitution stated that education was compulsory and free for all children. Today, Costa Rica has the highest literacy rate in Central America, with more than 90 percent of its people able to read and write.

Costa Ricans are proud, too, of their democratic traditions. The presidential election of 1890 is considered to be the first truly democratic election in Central America. Dictatorships and military coups, which change governments by force rather than by vote, have been rare in Costa Rica's history.

Costa Rica is the third-smallest nation in Central America. It is surrounded by countries that have known almost nothing but warfare and revolution since gaining independence from Spain early in the nineteenth century. While every kind of upheaval has raged around them, Costa Ricans have been firm in not taking sides. In 1948, Costa Rica abolished its army. The country's commitment to peace has led to its reputation as the "Switzerland of Central America."

Because of its stable background and democratic traditions, Costa Rica was chosen as the site for the InterAmerican

Court of Human Rights in 1979. The University of Peace, sponsored by the United Nations, has also been built in Costa Rica. The creation of that university fulfilled the dream of the Costa Rican family who donated the land. They wanted a university where courses would include the study of peace as a way of life, human rights, and issues such as energy and the environment.

Costa Ricans are conscious of the precious heritage they have in the land around them and in the magnificent richness and beauty of their forests, rivers, and coasts. To preserve this inheritance, they have established many national parks and reserves to protect the huge variety of animals and plants that live there. Because of Costa Rica's location in Central America, its wildlife represents a mix of North and South American species that evolved over thousands of years. Today, Costa Rica has twice as many species of trees as there are in the continental United States.

Costa Rica's Future

The great hope for the future is ecotourism, a new concept that encourages people to enjoy and learn more about the natural world. A successful ecotourist industry would be of great benefit to Costa Rica's economy. The nation is now well known for the diversity and richness of its natural parks and reserves, and an increasing number of visitors are arriving from around the world, eager to see the wealth of fauna and flora in this unique region. With continued careful management, its fascinating environment, along with the warmth and

Opposite: **The volcano Arenal releases plumes of smoke as viewed from Tabacon Hot Springs.**

friendship of its people, will make Costa Rica a popular destination for tourists for many years to come.

In a 1995 lecture given at the Royal Botanic Gardens at Kew, London, President José Figueres Ferrer summed up his government's plans for the use of land in Costa Rica. He would like to see the land area of the country devoted to

A cloud forest in Chirripó National Park

national parks and reserves increased from 25 to 50 percent. The remaining half of the land could be used for planting trees as a crop, for promoting agriculture, and for developing urban areas. These ideas, the president indicated, were only a beginning, but with international investment already attracted to the plan, Costa Rica looks forward to a bright future.

The Rich Coast

Costa Rica lies between Nicaragua to the north and Panama to the south. The Pacific Ocean is to the west and the Caribbean Sea to the east with the Atlantic Ocean beyond. The country covers an area of approximately 19,730 square miles (51,100 sq km), which makes it a little smaller than the state of West Virginia.

T HE GREATEST DISTANCE FROM NORTH TO south is 288 miles (463 km), and the country's narrowest width is 74 miles (120 km). After Panama, this is the shortest crossing of the Central American isthmus.

On several occasions, politicians and business leaders have discussed building another canal like the Panama Canal. The route they considered closely follows the San Juan River, which forms part of the border between Nicaragua and Costa Rica, but nothing has ever come of the suggestion.

An aerial view of Poás Volcano

Ring of Fire

Costa Rica is part of the so-called ring of fire, a line of volcanoes that roughly girdles the Pacific, so Costa Ricans are well used to earthquakes and tremors. Earthquakes and the uplifting of mountain ranges are caused by the shifting of the giant rocky plates that form the earth's shell. The friction between the plates produces the enormous heat seen in volcanoes.

This movement of the earth's plates has been occurring for millions of years since the time when, instead of seven conti-

Opposite: **Palms and driftwood on the beach in Cahuita National Park**

The Rich Coast **17**

The Pacific Ring of Fire

Volcanoes, Ring of Fire
Tectonic Plates

nents, there was just a single landmass—Pangaea. About 200 million years ago, Pangaea split into two separate landmasses, one in the north and the other in the south. Then, about 130 million years ago, the South American continent separated from the southern mass.

At first, a series of islands appeared between North and South America, allowing some animal and plant species to cross between continents. These islands probably appeared and disappeared several times until about 3 or 4 million years ago when the land connection between north and south was complete. Costa Rica is part of that major link between the continents of North America and South America, and for that reason, it is especially important to scientists.

Hurricanes

Hurricanes frequently appear off Costa Rica's coasts, occasionally causing great devastation. In 1996, Costa Rica was hit by two hurricanes. Hurricane César damaged coffee crops and killed more than forty people. Rains that accompanied Hurricane Douglas caused a landslide, killing ten people.

Geographical Features

Area: 19,730 square miles (51,100 sq km)

Highest Elevation: Chirripó Grande, 12,530 feet (3,819 m)

Lowest Elevation: Sea level along coasts

Longest River: San Juan River

Largest City: San José

Average Annual Precipitation: 100 inches (254 cm)

In tropical regions, the weather is usually hot and rainy. Costa Rica is a tropical land, but it has a varied climate, partly because of its rugged mountains. Night temperatures in the higher regions range from a high of 95° F (35° C) to below freezing.

Winds also affect the climate, and the Costa Ricans give them special names. The *norte* is a cool wind from North America that sometimes reaches Costa Rica between November and January, lowering temperatures for a few days. The *papagayos* are strong winds that blow in from the Pacific, and *alisios* are the trade winds that affect the northern slopes near the Pacific. Each of these winds creates a temporary weather change that may strongly affect some areas, such as northwestern Guanacaste.

A chain of mountains curves from the northwest to the southeast across Costa Rica. To the north are the *cordilleras*, mountain ranges, of Guanacaste and Tilarán. At the center is the Cordillera Central, and in the south stands the Cordillera de Talamanca. Costa Rica's highest mountain, Chirripó Grande, is on the western side of the Cordillera de Talamanca.

Hikers at the summit of Chirripó Grande

On clear days, you can see the Pacific Ocean and even the Atlantic Ocean from its summit at 12,530 feet (3,819 m).

Separating the Cordillera de Talamanca from the Pacific Ocean is a lower range of mountains known as the *Fila Costeña*, which literally means the "coastal row."

Between the Cordillera de Talamanca and the Fila Costeña lies a long fertile valley. The northern section of the valley, famed for its pineapples, coffee, and cattle, is known as the *Valle del General* (Valley of the General).

Costa Rica's longest river, the Río Grande de Térraba, rises in the Cordillera de Talamanca and runs through this valley, taking in many tributaries. These rivers and others from the slopes of the Fila Costeña carve their way westward to the Pacific.

On the Caribbean coast, there is a range of hills called the *Fila de Matama* with a highest point of 7,385 feet (2,251 m). The range almost reaches the sea near Puerto Limón, the major port on this coast.

The Meseta Central

The Cordillera Central overlooks the *Meseta Central* (Central Valley). The altitude of the meseta ranges from 3,000 to 4,000 feet (914 to 1,219 m) above sea level. The Meseta Central is the heartland of Costa Rica. In every direction, you can see forested slopes and rolling hills covered in lush, green coffee plants or tall stands of sugarcane. Small farms dot the landscape of cultivated fields. More than half of Costa Rica's people live in the valleys of the Meseta Central, with just over 300,000 in the capital city, San José.

Costa Rica's Meseta Central is home to coffee plantations and lush rolling hills.

Surrounded by low mountains, San José stands at an altitude of 3,773 feet (1,150 m) in the northern part of the Meseta Central. For much of the year, the climate is excellent, with springlike temperatures and some rain.

Costa Ricans talk about two seasons—the wet season, which is between May and November, and the dry season, which lasts for the rest of the year. Even during the wet sea-

San José, Costa Rica's capital city

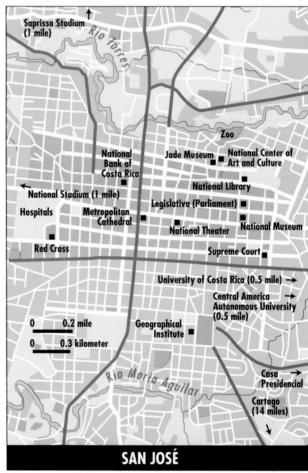

SAN JOSÉ

son, the sun usually shines until midday in San José, though you can sometimes see rainstorms forming over the mountains. Nestled in a valley, San José is protected by the mountains, so the city's average rainfall is only about 74 inches (190 cm) per year.

Because of the city's high altitude, the biggest change in temperature is between day and night, and some evenings can be quite chilly. As more and more people move into the city, the number of vehicles has increased, and today there is serious pollution and traffic congestion, particularly in the narrow streets. As a result, the clear air of San José has been damaged in recent years.

Not far from San José but at a higher altitude stands Cartago, Costa Rica's second city. Between the two, a range of hills known as La Carpintera marks the continental divide. This is the high point from which some rivers flow east to the Caribbean and others flow west to the Pacific.

One of the major rivers flowing east is the Reventazón. Adventurous tourists love to kayak down this turbulent river as it tumbles through gorges and dense forests to the coast.

From San José it is easy to see the volcanoes of Poás and Irazú. Poás is 8,872 feet (2,704 m) high while Irazú—at 11,260 feet (3,432 m)—is the highest volcano in Costa Rica. Nearby stands

The Reventazón River is a favorite of kayakers and rafters.

San José: Did You Know This?

When San José was settled in 1736, the tiny village was called *Villa Nueva de la Boca del Monte* (New Villa at the Mouth of the Mountain). It sits surrounded by volcanoes in the fertile basin of Meseta Central at 3,773 feet (1,150 m) above sea level. In 1823, San José replaced the city of Cartago as the country's capital, and today has a population of 318,756. It is home to the University of Costa Rica, the national theater, and a park named after U.S. president John F. Kennedy. The city celebrates the feast day of its patron saint, Saint Joseph, on March 19.

Cartago and Puerto Limón

Cartago stands at an altitude of 4,720 feet (1,439 m), only 14 miles (22.5 km) from San José in the southern and slightly higher valley of the Meseta Central. It has a population of 30,000. The town, which was founded in 1564 by Juan Vásquez de Coronado at the foot of the Irazú volcano, was the nation's capital until 1823. Twice in recent times its buildings have been severely damaged by earthquakes—in 1841 and in 1910. Many of the buildings that appear to be old have actually been rebuilt in Spanish colonial style. The church of *Nuestra Señora de Los Angeles* (Our Lady of the Angels), the patron of Costa Rica, was rebuilt in 1926 in a Byzantine style and houses a treasured image of the Virgin.

An American benefactor, Charles Lankester, left to the people of Costa Rica some land near Cartago along with his collection of plants. The Lankester Gardens, as the area is known today, houses many hundreds of species of orchids and bromeliads. The gardens, now in the care of the University of Costa Rica, are visited by flower lovers from all over the world.

On the Caribbean coast, Limón, or Puerto Limón, has a population of more than 56,000. As Costa Rica's most important port, it services the principal banana-growing area in the lowlands. The port developed with the construction of the Atlantic railway in the late 1870s and the growth of the banana industry. Today,

the port facility has been largely transferred to a new terminal at Moín. The town has a palm-fringed promenade and a green, tropical park frequented by two-toed sloths—curiously sluggish animals native to Central and South America.

Turrialba, the second-highest volcano at 10,650 feet (3,246 m), and dormant Barba at 9,534 feet (2,906 m) surrounded by the forests of Braulio Carrillo National Park. Some of the nation's more than sixty volcanoes have been extinct for a long time, while others show signs of activity ranging from modest puffs of steam to spectacular explosions of rock and fire.

Flowers flourish in close proximity to the active volcano Poás.

Earthquake Safety Rules

A newspaper published these safety suggestions for Costa Ricans:

DO

- When the shaking starts, get to a doorway, an inside corner wall, or under a desk or table.
- Disconnect the electricity as soon as you can, safely, to avoid fire. Take pots off stove.
- If you are driving, stop. You could hit a panicky pedestrian running blindly into the street. Get out of the car and seek shelter in a doorway.

DON'T

- Don't rush outside. Outside walls tend to fall outward; windows shatter; trees, poles, and signs topple; roof tiles fall into the street; and power lines come down.
- Don't use the telephone. Lines must be kept open for ambulances, fire trucks, and other emergency services.
- Don't use elevators or escalators right after a quake.

The Pacific Coast

For almost the whole length of the Pacific coast, hilly slopes descend straight to the sea. However, a narrow strip of land lies between the sea and the mountain foothills in the northern area of Guanacaste. Much of that land is used to raise cattle.

The major port on this side for many years was Puntarenas. It was built on a spit of land about 3 miles (5 km) long, backed by a wall of mountains. Puntarenas is no longer important as a port, its

Volcanic Eruptions and Earthquakes

Cartago has been severely damaged by earthquakes three times—in 1620, in 1841, and in 1910, when the worst earthquake in Costa Rica's history left 1,750 people dead. Much of San José was covered in ash in 1963 when Irazú erupted for the first time in twenty years.

In 1968, the eruption of Arenal Volcano, in the Cordillera de Tilarán, hurled large blocks of volcanic rock up to 3 miles (5 km). The eruption devastated farmland and killed many people and cattle. Arenal erupted again in 1993 and 1998.

After an earthquake on April 22, 1991, Puerto Limón on the Caribbean coast was about 3 feet (1 m) higher above the sea than it had been. The city's highway to San José was destroyed, and the town was isolated for several days. Inland roads suffered landslides, and shocks were felt for weeks afterward.

place having been taken by Caldera, which is newer. But the land around Puntarenas provides a living for people who raise cattle and grow bananas, rice, and coconuts.

The Pacific coastline is much longer than it seems on a map because of its many peninsulas and bays. In the far north is the Santa Elena Peninsula; then comes the largest peninsula, Nicoya, which can be reached either by road or ferry from Puntarenas. Its many miles of sandy beaches make

Mountain foothills lead to the Pacific Ocean.

Fishing boats harbor at Puntarenas.

Nicoya a favorite with tourists. Parts of the central southern region of the Nicoya Peninsula reach altitudes of more than 3,000 feet (914 m).

In southwest Costa Rica, the Osa Peninsula is smaller, and Puerto Jiménez is the only town of any size. On the west side of the peninsula is Corcovado National Park. Punta Burica in the far south is shared with Panama. These many peninsulas, together with numerous small bays, make the Pacific coastline almost 630 miles (1,015 km) long.

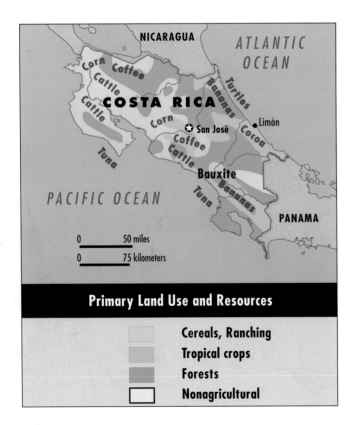

Primary Land Use and Resources

- Cereals, Ranching
- Tropical crops
- Forests
- Nonagricultural

The Caribbean Coast

By contrast, the Caribbean coast is only 185 miles (298 km) long. A large triangular area of lowland plains stretches inland from the Caribbean to the border with Nicaragua in the north and to the mountains in the west. These plains, or *llanuras*, are named Guatuso, San Carlos, Tortuguero, and Santa Clara. Their altitude seldom exceeds 328 feet (100 m), and together they cover approximately 20 percent of Costa Rica's land area.

There are few good beaches on the Caribbean coast and swimming is not recommended. These waters have strong currents—and sharks.

Unlike the Caribbean coast, the Pacific coast has many islands. Near the Nicaraguan border, the Isla Bolaños is dry and scrub covered, a home to many seabirds. The Isla Chira in the Gulf of Nicoya, between the peninsula and the mainland, is a larger island with a hill 824 feet (251 m) high. Other islands in the same gulf include Isla Tortuga and San Lucas, which was once used as a prison. The nearby islets of Guayabo and Negritos are biological reserves.

The Isla del Coco is a little more than 300 miles (480 km) to the southwest on a latitude that crosses the South American mainland. The island is approximately 7.5 miles long and 3 miles wide (12 by 5 km). Juan Cabezas, a navigator and sea

Wafer Bay on Isla del Coco

A Film Set

Perhaps the Isla del Coco's greatest claim to fame is its selection as the location for parts of Steven Spielberg's film *Jurassic Park* (1993). Watch for the emerald green island in the opening sequences!

captain who landed in 1526, is thought to have been the first European to discover it.

At the western end, the land rises abruptly to Yglesias Hill, the highest point. Pirates and early explorers are said to have used the hill as a lookout, and there are many rumors and stories of treasure buried here. Dozens of treasure hunters have tried their luck, but so far nothing has been found.

No one lives on Isla del Coco, making it possibly the world's largest uninhabited island. During the early twentieth century, a few people brought pigs, planted coffee, and tried to settle there—but unsuccessfully. The land is not easy to farm, being rocky and hilly, heavily wooded, and having more than 200 waterfalls.

Today, it is very expensive to get to the island, and only a few visitors and scientists go to see the wildlife. This small island has been set aside as a biological reserve. Of special interest are some species of plants and animals found only on the island, including three birds: the Coco Island cuckoo, the Coco Island finch, and the ridgeway flycatcher.

The Land of National Parks

At one time, much of Costa Rica was covered with forests of many types, including rain forests. However, human activity has destroyed large areas of these forests.

Previous page:
**A strangler fig
tree in La Amistad
International Park**

ENVIRONMENTALISTS WORLDWIDE ARE CONCERNED ABOUT the destruction of the rain forests. It is particularly important in Costa Rica because of the nation's position between North America and South America, and because the land has such a variety of animals and plants.

Destruction of the Forests

In 1950, the population of Costa Rica was nearly 900,000. Between 1950 and 1961, forest clearance in Costa Rica was a modest 139 square miles (360 sq km) per year. Since that time, the population has tripled, and forest clearance has also increased. By the early 1980s, 322 square miles (835 sq km) of forests were being cut down each year. By 1988, the rate had slowed, but even at an estimated 193 square miles (500 sq km) per year, approximately 4 percent of the remaining forest was being cut annually. By comparison with the cutting of the Amazon rain forest, the area is small, but Costa Rica is a tiny country.

This destruction of forests is partly a result of the increase in population, and partly because Costa Rica needed to increase its exports, which are mainly agricultural. Costa Rica, like many Latin American countries, hoped to improve its economy by cultivating more crops and using cleared rain forest to raise cattle. Between 1965 and 1988, the nation's coffee exports increased by 300 percent, and many thousands of live cattle were exported every year.

This terraced hillside is home to a coffee plantation.

Saving the Forests

Luckily for the Costa Ricans, some politicians, environmentalists, and landowners decided to turn much of the remaining forestland into protected parks and reserves. The land included forests of many kinds as well as wetlands, beaches, and other regions that were of special interest to scientists or naturalists.

The result has been that almost 25 percent of Costa Rica is now protected land. Based on percentages, this is the highest rate among Western nations, so Costa Rica is rightly known as the "land of national parks."

The wealth of natural species in Costa Rica is easily seen in a tour of a forested mountainside. At each level the rainfall,

The National Tree

The guanacaste, the national tree of Costa Rica, is well adapted to dry conditions. The province in the northwest of Costa Rica is named after this tree. Often called the elephant's ear or monkey ear, it gets its nickname from the brown ear-shaped seed pods that dangle high in the tree. The pods are used as cattle food, and the seeds can be eaten.

National Parks and Reserves

temperature, sunlight, and soil vary, so the plants at the top are different from those found at the bottom.

Of course, each kind of vegetation attracts certain species of animals, and it is not only the mammals that are different. Birds, reptiles, amphibians, insects, and others form a web of life in which each part depends on another for survival.

The Highest Park

Chirripó National Park south of San José includes Costa Rica's highest peak, Cerro Chirripó Grande. Also among its many wonders are lakes formed thousands of years ago when the land was scoured by glaciers. In the highest places around these lakes, the vegetation consists of alpine-type *páramo* grasslands and boggy areas. The plants are mostly small and resistant to heavy rainfall and low temperatures. Lower down

Opposite: **Cerro Chirripó Grande is a very popular tourist destination.**

The Quetzal

One gorgeous bird found in the cooler, higher forest is the rare resplendent quetzal. This spectacular bird, which belongs to the trogon family, has a glittering plumage of blue and green and a crimson-colored stomach. It was greatly revered by the Maya people of ancient Central America and is part of their mythology. The quetzal is found not only in the Chirripó area but also in forests from southern Mexico to western Panama. In many places, this beautiful bird is in danger because its habitat is threatened by loggers and farmers.

the slopes, the vegetation changes according to the rainfall and altitude.

There is a range of forests, including mixed forests of trees that keep their leaves and trees that do not, as well as oak forests, valleys green with ferns, and cloud-soaked rain forests. In the cloud forests, every tree seems to be covered with mosses, small ferns, colorful orchids, or bromeliads.

At each level of the mountain slope, the birds are different. The variety is enormous, ranging from the tiniest hummingbirds that hover over flowers with an almost invisible beating of wings to magnificent eagles.

Among the mammals of this mountain park are several members of the cat family, such as the margay. The margay is a small animal about the size of a house cat, with dark markings on a light brown coat. Other residents include pumas (otherwise known as cougars or mountain lions), ocelots, and jaguars—the largest of Central American carnivores.

The margay cat is native to Costa Rica and other Central American countries.

The "Friendliest" Park

La Amistad International Park, Costa Rica's largest but least accessible park, covers 479,000 acres (193,845 ha). This park is a joint project between Costa Rica and Panama that expresses *amistad* (friendship) and cooperation in the cause of environmental protection. Much of the park is high in the Cordillera de Talamanca, and the plants and animals are similar to those in the Chirripó.

The Amistad Park, much of which has yet to be explored, has already revealed almost 400 different species of birds. Scientists also believe the park has the largest concentration of quetzals in Costa Rica. Amistad is very popular with hikers and backpackers, who wander the trails always hoping to spot a new species.

A dramatic waterfall in La Amistad International Park

The Deepest Park

The Barra Honda National Park, about 208 miles (335 km) northwest of San José, extends into more than forty underground caverns in the dry northwest of the country. This is a small park by comparison with Chirripó, but it is geologically important. The hollowed rock was once part of a marine coral reef, and the deepest cavern so far explored is 790 feet (240 m) below the earth's surface. Bats, blind salamanders, and fish as well as cave insects and specialized plants live in the darkness of the caverns.

Barra Honda is surrounded by forests of wild plum and wild cotton. Aboveground, the forest is home to white-nosed coatis—racoonlike mammals—and white-faced capuchin monkeys, skunks, and armadillos. Among the many birds are orange-fronted parakeets of the parrot family.

The white-faced capuchin monkey, one of hundreds of species found in Barra Honda National Park

Beaches

Almost more beautiful than the forests are the beaches that line Osa Peninsula in the southwest. The Corcovado National Park, one of Costa Rica's most spectacular parks, was established here in the 1970s.

Corcovado is extremely isolated and includes the only truly virgin rain forest left in Central America. Early in the twentieth century, the area was considered so remote that it became a kind of penal colony, a place where people were sent for punishment. They survived by hacking down trees, growing a few crops, fishing, and panning the rivers for gold.

Corcovado Park's amazing variety of wildlife includes scarlet macaws, jacamars, humming-birds, harpy eagles, white-lipped peccaries—wild pigs—as well as jaguars, giant anteaters, sloths, and squirrel monkeys. And that is just a partial list. The park is a veritable storehouse of Central American natural history. Who knows how many secrets or undiscovered species still hide within its forests?

Other parks with fine beaches are Cabo Blanco Reserve at the southern tip of the Nicoya Peninsula, and tiny Manuel Antonio National Park south of San José, popular for its miles of fine white sand. You have to wade across a shallow estuary to reach the beaches, but it is well worth the effort.

The three-toed sloth *(above)* **and the scarlet macaw** *(left)*

Saving the Turtles

At the same time every year, thousands of marine turtles return to the beach on which they were hatched to nest and lay their eggs. These mass migrations are threatened by poachers who kill the turtles for their eggs, oil, and shells. In the 1970s, Costa Rica began a program to save the turtles. Now, during the *arribadas* (arrivals in port), as the gatherings of turtles are called, the beaches are protected day and night.

The beaches of the National Park of Santa Rosa in the northwest are also important. Two of Santa Rosa's beaches are well-known nesting sites for turtles, and the tiny Nancite beach is visited by thousands of Pacific ridley turtles every year.

From Moín, on the Caribbean coast near Puerto Limón, a series of canals just inland from the sea run northwest to Barra del Colorado. These canals were built to connect many of the natural lagoons along the swampy coastline and are still used by barges to transport bananas and other goods. The lagoons and canals are home to sea cows or manatees, large mammals that live on water plants and never leave the water. Some of the lagoons and large stretches of the beaches have been set aside as the National Park of Tortuguero. *Tortuguero*

These canals are used by barges to transport bananas and other products.

means "turtle catcher." These beaches are the most important nesting places in the western Caribbean for the endangered green turtle.

The low ground inland from the sea is part of the Llanura de Tortuguero, where some of Costa Rica's most ancient rain forests have been set aside as a national wildlife refuge. Here the annual rainfall reaches 240 inches (610 cm). Luckily, these rain forests and their tremendous variety of animals and plants have been safe from human activity thus far because they are accessible only by boat or aircraft. But loggers and developers have now carved trails across the plains right to the edge of the refuge, cutting down some of the country's finest forests on the way.

A Wealth of Wildlife

Official statistics show that Costa Rica's parks protect an astonishing variety of wildlife, including the following:

849 species of resident birds

several hundred species of visiting birds

205 species of mammals

160 species of amphibians

218 species of reptiles

130 species of freshwater fish

1,200 species of classified orchids (and hundreds more yet to be listed)

more than 900 species of ferns

10 percent of all the butterfly species in the world

The Monteverde Cloud Forest Reserve

More than fifty areas in Costa Rica have been set aside by the government as national parks, reserves, and refuges. In addition, several areas are protected by individuals or not-for-profit foundations.

Monteverde Cloud Forest Reserve is the best known of the privately run areas. Its story began in 1951 when some North American Quakers, mainly from Alabama, settled in a remote section of the Tilarán mountain range. At that time, there were no roads, and it took several days by oxcart to get to San José, about 112 miles (180 km) away.

The immigrants cleared some land and built homes, a meetinghouse, and a school. They soon found that the land was good for raising dairy cattle and, within a few years, they built their first cheese factory. Today, their cheese is sold all over the country, and it is also exported. The community dairy factory and shop are now very much a part of Costa Rican life.

In 1986, residents and visiting conservationists founded the Monteverde Conservation League. It protects a large area of cloud forest, where the trees are almost permanently shrouded in mist. Streams and waterfalls tumble down the slopes, which are thick with mosses, ferns, bromeliads, lianas, epiphytic plants (growing on trees), vines, orchids, and many colorful flowers.

Small frogs, spiders, leaf-cutting ants, and many other insects live on the dark, damp forest floor where the air can be quite cold because there is almost no sunlight. More than 400

species of birds, the quetzal among them, have been found in Monteverde, along with some 500 species of butterflies, 100 mammal species, and more than 2,000 kinds of plants.

The Monteverde Reserve, now Costa Rica's number-one tourist attraction, has become a special place for research students and scientists. Of the many thousands of visitors who come, some stay to work in the reserve. Nearby, though less well known, is the Reserva Santa Elena, also in the cloud forest, and *El Bosque Eterno de los Niños* (the Children's Eternal Rain Forest), which was established with funds raised by schoolchildren from many parts of the world.

Opposite: **Monteverde Cloud Forest Reserve**

Leaf-cutting ants carry home the fruits of their labors.

CHAPTER FOUR

A History of Freedom

The first people in the region of Costa Rica probably lived about 10,000 years ago. They survived by fishing, hunting, and gathering fruit and nuts from the forests.

THE OLDEST POTTERY IN COSTA RICA dates from about 1000–500 B.C. Communities at that time seem to have been well organized, especially those in the north, having chiefs, nobles, and priests. Towns were constructed around a central plaza or main square. Most people worked on the land, producing corn (maize), beans, squash, and cotton.

Archaeologists have not found any large monuments in Costa Rica, such as the pyramids built by the Maya and Toltec civilizations in southern Mexico and northern Guatemala. It is clear, though, that the people of Costa Rica had contact with the Maya, and also with tribes from Panama and Colombia. Costa Rica was on the trading route between these two regions.

When the Europeans arrived in Costa Rica in the sixteenth century, an estimated 27,000 people lived in the region. The most populated area was the present-day province of Guanacaste, where the Chorotega and other Nicoyan tribes cultivated crops such as corn and beans.

Ancient clay pottery in the form of a bird

Opposite: **Jade pendant**

Mystery of the Stone Balls

Dotted around the Diquis region in southwest Costa Rica are some large stone balls that are probably about 1,000 years old. They are perfectly round, and some stand more than 6 feet (2 m) high. These balls are made of very hard granite and are found in random places. To date, they remain a mystery to archaeologists. How did the ancient peoples carve such perfect spheres, and why?

The Catapa, Voto, and Suerre peoples lived in the north, the Cabecar and Bribrí in the southern Talamanca range, and the Térraba and Boruca in the Diquis Valley. These tribes were constantly at war with one another, but no all-powerful group emerged. When the Spaniards arrived, the native peoples put up fierce resistance. Many fled to the forests and highlands, continuing to attack the Spaniards long after the conquest.

Discovery and Conquest

Christopher Columbus arrived in Costa Rica in 1502. Almost twenty years later, the Spaniard Gil González Davila explored most of the length of the Pacific coast on foot. Shortly afterward, Francisco Fernández de Córdova founded the first Spanish settlement in Costa Rica near the present-day port of Puntarenas.

For many years, Spanish expeditions stayed close to the coast, and it was almost forty years before they began exploring the

ATLANTIC OCEAN

PACIFIC OCEAN

0   50 miles
0   75 kilometers

Voyages of Discovery, 1502–1564

—— Columbus 1502–1503
—— Juan de Cavallón, 1561
—— Vásquez de Coronado, 1564

interior. In 1559, King Philip II of Spain wanted the area populated with Spanairds and the Indians converted to Christianity. (The people had come to be known as "Indians" because when Columbus and other explorers reached the Americas, they mistakenly thought they had arrived in the East Indies.) Spanish settlements were to be built well inland to make them safe from pirates. Anyone successful in this mission would be well rewarded by the king with land and Indian slaves.

King Philip II of Spain

A young lawyer named Juan de Cavallón was charged with settling the interior of the country. In January 1561, he set out from Nicaragua with ninety soldiers and an assortment of domestic animals. Three months later, he founded Castillo de Garcimuñoz, the first Spanish settlement in present-day Costa Rica. He was followed by Juan Vásquez de Coronado, who transferred the settlement to Cartago, which he founded in 1564. Many consider Coronado to be the first true conqueror of Costa Rica. He was a wise man who used his power well. He made friends with the native people and had some control over them. At the same time, he welcomed Spanish settlers, who brought cattle, horses, and pigs with them. He was drowned at sea in 1573 while returning to Spain to seek more funds for the small colony.

Colonization

Costa Rica lost its attraction for the Spanish after they discovered there was little chance of finding gold and other minerals there. So, left to its own devices, the country devel-

After the arrival of the Spanish, many Native Americans fled into the forests.

Cacao beans were used as currency for nearly two centuries.

oped slowly. Some Spanish colonists remained to work the land. Rather than become slaves, many Native Americans fled into the dense forests. Thousands of others died of various diseases brought by the Europeans, such as influenza and smallpox.

As a result, Spanish families, who settled mainly around the Meseta Central, were forced to work their own land. They grew maize, wheat, sugarcane, cacao, tobacco, beans, and cassava. They also raised cattle, horses, and pigs. Their lands and houses were often raided by fierce bands of Miskito Indians from Nicaragua, who destroyed the crops and plantations.

People who settled on the coast did not fare much better. Constant raids by French, Dutch, and English pirates had a devastating effect. The settlers were also subjected to heavy taxes imposed by the Spanish Crown. These were generally paid in cacao beans, which in 1709 became the "coin of the realm" and remained so until late in the nineteenth century.

In 1723, the volcano Irazú erupted, covering the capital city of Cartago in ash. At that time, the town had only seventy adobe houses, two churches, and two chapels. The new capital, San José, was founded in 1737, and Alajuela, not far from San José, in 1782. But Costa Rica's population of fewer than 20,000 remained poor. There were no medical facilities and few roads. Families had to survive on the food they produced, and on their isolated farms, colonists had little contact with one another.

Its lack of mineral wealth, however, saved Costa Rica from the greed and violence that devastated other colonies. Most important, the landholding families developed as a single group, which many believe laid the basis for the peaceful and democratic nature of today's Costa Rican society.

In colonial Costa Rica, there was no place for social classes, power-hungry officials, or even hatred of the Spanish administration. But these problems existed everywhere else in Central America and ultimately led to the demand for independence from Spain. The small, backward colony of Costa Rica was swept along in the tide of events.

The United Provinces of Central America

Mexico gained its independence from Spain in August 1821, and the Central American republics followed one month later. Soon after, General Agustín de Iturbide, who had made himself emperor of Mexico, tried to include Costa Rica in his empire.

Not all Costa Ricans agreed. The conservative-minded people of Heredia and Cartago supported the idea, but the people of San José and Alajuela, favoring complete independence, did not. The "independents" won and made San José the country's capital in place of Cartago. In 1823, Costa Rica joined the other Central American

Mexico and Central America in 1830

United Provinces of
Central America 1823–1838

republics to form a federation, the United Provinces of Central America.

The federation lasted until 1838, but the Central American republics were often involved in disputes and strife. In 1824, Guanacaste, then part of Nicaragua, had asked to become part of Costa Rica. The federation agreed, but the boundary remained a matter of dispute between the two countries until 1896.

A New Republic

Long before the Central American federation collapsed, Costa Rica had its first constitution, which laid down the laws for governing the country. Juan Mora Fernández was elected the first president and remained in office until 1833. He was largely responsible for introducing coffee into Costa Rica, where it became a great commercial success.

But it was also a stroke of luck that really got the coffee industry going. In the 1840s, English merchant William Le Lacheur arrived in Puntarenas looking for some cargo to take home on his ship, the *Monarch*. He filled his ship with coffee beans, promising to return in two years to pay for them. The coffee was a great success in Europe, and Le Lacheur became a wealthy man. Soon British companies began to invest in the Costa Rican coffee industry.

The promotion of the coffee industry was also a priority of dictator Braulio Carrillo, president from 1835 to 1837 and from 1838 to 1842. President Carrillo was a good administrator. He introduced new legal codes to replace the out-of-date Spanish laws and led the way toward reforming land ownership. But he was also a harsh dictator who would not tolerate criticism, especially when it came from towns outside San José.

In time, his enemies conspired against him, inviting General Francisco Morazán of Honduras, the last president of the Central American federation, to join them. Morazán's dream was a union of the Central American republics, and he still hoped he could re-create the federation. He deposed and exiled Carrillo and made himself president of Costa Rica. However, Morazán faced bitter opposition when he tried to introduce military conscription and impose taxes. He was forced from office and executed in 1842.

Coffee quickly became one of Costa Rica's major crops.

Francisco Morazán, the last president of the Central American federation

William Walker

The only time Costa Rica has been involved in an international war was between 1856 and 1858. The president of the country was Juan Rafael Mora, a coffee planter, who fixed the elections during his first term so that he could stay in power. It is unlikely that Congress would have allowed him to stay had it not been for the ambitions of William Walker of Tennessee. Walker was a filibuster, one of a group of men who became illegally involved in a foreign war.

In 1855, Walker was invited to join one side during a civil war in Nicaragua. He arrived with his private army, quickly took control of the Nicaraguan armed forces, and declared himself president of that country. Among those who opposed this move was American magnate Cornelius Vanderbilt, whose Accessory Transit Company ran a steamship and carriage operation in Nicaragua.

Walker was in a shaky position, but he was rescued by some North American slave traders who offered him men, arms, and money on condition that he introduce slavery into Nicaragua. Walker agreed and continued with the second stage of his plan, which was to hand over the weak nations of Central America to his supporters as part of a Confederacy of Southern American States. With this goal in mind, he invaded Costa Rica in March 1856.

Costa Ricans responded readily to a call to arms, and with an army of some 9,000 men, President Mora successfully ousted Walker. He then pursued Walker's men into Nicaragua, forcing them to retreat even farther in the Battle of Rivas. A great many Costa Rican soldiers died at Rivas, and Juan Santamaría, a drummer boy, became a national hero when he set fire to an enemy stronghold before he was fatally shot.

President Mora was welcomed back as a national hero. Walker continued his activities in other parts of Central America until 1860, when he was executed by a Honduran firing squad.

San José, 1859

By the mid-nineteenth century, Costa Rican society had changed, largely because of the prosperity brought by the coffee industry. But not everyone benefited from this prosperity, and Costa Rican society became divided between rich and poor. The wealthy coffee industry families created an oligarchy—a small group of people who use power for their own benefit. They controlled all the important political posts, even that of the presidency.

The Guardia Dictatorship

After a successful coup in 1870, General Tomás Guardia seized power and established a military dictatorship. He was violently opposed to the upper-class coffee barons. He reduced their power by sending their leaders into exile and disbanding their political parties. He dissolved Congress and in 1871 created a new constitution that set down the rules by which the country was governed. This constitution lasted until 1949. But Guardia put his own friends and relatives into important positions and used his power ruthlessly.

Despite his lasting reputation as a harsh dictator, Guardia also pursued some liberal ideas. He levied high taxes but used the money for the widespread construction of schools and improvements in public-health facilities. Under his regime, and well ahead of many other countries in the Americas, capital punishment was abolished.

He is perhaps best remembered, though, as the president who inaugurated the railroad from San José to Puerto Limón, which was used for transporting coffee from the highlands to the Caribbean coast.

Bananas

Costa Rica was the first Central American country to cultivate bananas. They grew well on the Caribbean coastal plains, but it was a region of swamps and tropical jungle where few people lived. A great deal of money had to be invested to develop the land and build houses, schools, and health facilities for the workers.

The Jungle Train

The man responsible for the construction of the railroad was an American named Minor Cooper Keith. He was the nephew of Henry Meiggs, also an American, who built the first railroads in Chile and in the Peruvian Andes.

At first, progress was very slow because many workers fell ill with malaria, yellow fever, and dysentery. When Keith had difficulty persuading the Costa Ricans to work in the hot, wet lowlands on the Caribbean coast, he brought in Chinese and Italian labor. Eventually, he brought thousands of black West Indians from the British Caribbean islands to complete the task.

The first 25 miles (40 km) of track follows the coast through rows of coconut palms and then turns inland across swamps. It is said that 4,000 workers died during the construction. But the railroad made Keith a very wealthy man, and he invested large sums in the banana business.

An early photo showing bananas being carried to market

The Costa Rican coffee barons had little interest in the banana business. As a result, the Caribbean banana industry was controlled largely by foreigners and had little to do with the rest of the country. Previously, Great Britain had been a leading investor in Costa Rica, but now it was North America's turn. Toward the end of the century, American businessman Minor Cooper Keith's interests and plantations merged with those of other foreigners to become the United Fruit Company, one of the most successful industries in Costa Rica for many years.

Changing Times

President José Joaquín Rodriguez

Toward the end of the nineteenth century, the spread of liberal and democratic ideas brought political change in Costa Rica. Although the average citizen had little interest in the political process, candidates for the presidency in 1889 actively sought their support.

Until this time, the election of the president was controlled by an elite minority of Costa Ricans, and when the president who was in power tried to impose his own candidate, angry peasants marched into San José and

COSTA RICA

Cerro Pando

Golfito

PANAMA

Península de Oso

PACIFIC OCEAN

ATLANTIC OCEAN

0   20 miles

0   32 kilometers

Costa Rica–Panama, 1802–1941

— Current borders

— Claimed by Panama

Border Disputes

The beginning of the twentieth century saw Costa Rica in border disputes with both Nicaragua and Panama. Without consulting Costa Rica, Nicaragua agreed that the United States could build a canal across the isthmus. The canal would cross not only Nicaraguan territory but also the San Juan River on the border with Costa Rica. A judgment made in Costa Rica's favor by a Central American court was ignored by the United States and Nicaragua. However, that canal was never built.

The dispute with Panama concerned an area of the Caribbean coast. In 1900, a French president ruled that the land belonged to Panama. Fourteen years later, the chief justice of the U.S. Supreme Court judged in favor of Costa Rica. When the two sides tried to resolve the matter by armed conflict, the United States intervened, and the Panamanians were forced out of the territory. The dispute was finally resolved in 1941 when Costa Rica gained most of the territory.

forced the candidate to withdraw. The subsequent victory in 1890 of President José Joaquín Rodriguez is considered to be the first entirely free and honest election in Central America.

Democracy and Dictators

Two men dominated Costa Rican politics in the early twentieth century—Cleto González Víquez, who was president from 1906 to 1910 and again from 1928 to 1932, and Ricardo Jiménez Oreamuno, who was president from 1910 to 1914, from 1924 to 1928, and from 1932 to 1936.

Although they were political opponents, the two men shared many of the same ideals. They built more schools and provided better living and working conditions for the people. They also built more roads and bought back land from the United Fruit Company, which they then distributed to the poor.

The next president, Alfred González Flores, tried to improve the tax system but incurred the wrath of large planters and businesspeople who plotted against him to ensure he was not reelected. However, before they could act, the Tinoco brothers, Federico (who was minister of war) and Joaquín, ousted González Flores in a 1917 coup. The Tinocos seized power but became very unpopular when they curtailed the freedom of the press and jailed many political opponents.

Federico Tinoco

The Costa Ricans, unwilling to tolerate such behavior, took to the streets. Schoolteachers, including many women, and high school students led the way and set fire to the pro-Tinoco newspaper plant. Government troops retaliated but made the mistake of firing into the U.S. consulate where some of the protestors were hiding. The United States, which had never recognized the Tinoco regime, then threatened to intervene. Before this could happen and another coup could take place, Congress allowed the Tinocos to go into exile. This kind of dictatorship has never been repeated in Costa Rica.

Most people in Costa Rica, though, were still extremely poor. In 100 years, the population had increased from about 80,000 to more than 600,000. West Indians and others were brought in to work on the railway, immigrants came from Europe, and refugees arrived from other Central American countries.

A great many of these newcomers were unemployed, housing was scarce, workers were badly paid, and many people were ill and undernourished. The Costa Ricans demanded a solution to these problems, and they had the backing of several political parties, including the Communist Party.

The 1940 elections were won by Rafael Angel Calderón Guardia of the National Republican Party (PRN). He introduced far-reaching social reforms and a new labor code, which gave workers many rights and ensured that the state would provide for most of their needs, especially if they were ill or unemployed. His reforms were unique and well in advance of anything known in the region at that time. But when he turned to the Communists for support, Costa Rica's business leaders opposed him. Calderón also lost favor with middle-class intellectuals, who accused him of corruption and fraud.

His two leading opponents were Otilio Ulate Blanco, a newspaper publisher, and José Figueres Ferrer, a wealthy, liberal landowner. In 1942, Figueres made a radio broadcast fiercely critical of President Calderón. He was immediately seized and sent into exile for two years. He returned to Costa Rica determined that the only answer to Costa Rica's, and Central America's, problems was military rebellion.

Ulate ran against Calderón in the 1948 elections. The election took place against a background of assassinations and street fighting. Finally, the opposition parties organized a general strike of all the nation's workers. Figueres, convinced that the elections would be rigged, approached the president of Guatemala for help in supplying arms. When the ballots were counted, Ulate had 10,000 more votes than Calderón but, as the opposition had predicted, Congress did not recognize his victory.

President-elect Rafael Angel Calderón Guardia (with his wife) on a goodwill trip to the United States in 1940.

Publisher Otilio Ulate Blanco works on a campaign speech.

Civil War

The civil war that followed was the worst political crisis in Costa Rica's history. Figueres led the antigovernment forces, backed by arms and men from other Central American countries. His rebels gained control of Cartago and Puerto Limón and eventually surrounded San José.

The government's forces were poorly trained, and much of the fighting was left to the Communists. Many people died, and when there appeared to be a threat of U.S. intervention, the government capitulated. Calderón fled the country with some of his followers.

A junta (a group of people controlling a government) was formed and led by Figueres. It governed for eighteen months, during which time Congress ratified Ulate's position and drew up a new constitution by which the country has since been governed.

"Don Pepe" Figueres

José "Don Pepe" Figueres Ferrer was born in 1906, soon after his parents arrived in Costa Rica from Spain. He studied engineering in the United States in the 1920s. Back in Costa Rica, he bought a farm, which he called *La Lucha sin Fin*, meaning "the struggle without an end." It seems a strange name for a farm, but most of Don Pepe's work involved experimenting with new agricultural techniques and products. He also set up a scheme that gave his workers an opportunity to profit from the farm.

In 1953, he was elected president, achieving a stunning victory by winning 65 percent of the vote. His party, the PLN, also won a majority of the seats in the Legislative Assembly.

In power from 1953 to 1958 and again from 1970 to 1974, Don Pepe had an immense influence on national politics over several decades. Above all, he ensured that Costa Rica's democratic traditions were firmly established.

Writer, philosopher, engineer, politician, and the Father of Costa Rica, as he was affectionately known, Don Pepe died in 1990 at the age of eighty-three.

More Upheaval

In 1955, rebel exiles supporting former president Rafael Angel Calderón crossed from Nicaragua into northern Costa Rica. They were backed by the dictator leaders of Cuba, the Dominican Republic, Venezuela, and Colombia, as well as Nicaragua.

The rebels strafed San José, but President Don Pepe Figueres—with an army of 6,000 volunteers, including many high school students—repelled them. Rafael Angel Calderón ran for president again in 1962 but was unsuccessful. Since then, there have been no more threats of such uprisings.

From the 1970s to the 1990s

When Don Pepe Figueres left the presidency in 1974, after his second elected term, the country was greatly in debt to foreign banks and organizations. Under presidents Daniel Oduber and Rodrigo Carazo Odio, Costa Rica's economic problems increased. Many people were unemployed. Those who had jobs found that because of high inflation, the money they earned was not enough to pay for the goods they needed. Eventually, workers on the banana plantations, medical staff, and railway and dock workers went on strike.

Nobel Prizewinner

Oscar Arias Sánchez came from a wealthy Costa Rican family and studied economics at the University of Costa Rica. He later received a Ph.D. from the University of Essex in England. From 1972 to 1977, he was minister of planning in the national government. In 1979, he was elected secretary-general of the PLN. In 1986, at age forty-six, he was elected president and remained in office until 1990.

During his term as president, he was awarded the 1987 Nobel Peace Prize for his efforts to bring peace to the Central American region.

In 1982, Luis Alberto Monge Alvarez of the *Partido de Liberación Nacional* (PLN) was elected president. Having had experience in labor legislation and as a cabinet member, he negotiated an extension on the country's debts.

In return, he agreed to impose severe austerity measures. These included a devaluation of the currency, a reduction in government spending, and tax increases. He faced great opposition in imposing these measures as more and more people became unemployed. There were disturbances in the cities and a prolonged strike by the workers on the banana plantations. The troubles continued under the presidency of Oscar Arias Sánchez, the PLN leader.

The price of gasoline increased by 30 percent in the early 1990s.

During 1988 and 1989, strikes and protests by public employees and agricultural workers continued. At the same time, several leading political and business people were alleged to be involved in drug trafficking and had to resign.

A sharp decline in support for the PLN led to the election in 1990 of Angel Calderón Fournier, candidate of the Social Christian Unity Party (PUSC), as president. The party also won a majority in the assembly.

Inheriting a massive debt, Calderón had little choice but to continue the austerity program, which included a 30 percent increase in the price of gasoline and a 20 percent increase in other items. In a one-day general strike, workers gathered to protest the government's proposed tax increases. Calderón's government, too, became involved in allegations concerning drug money.

The PLN was returned to power in 1994 with the election of José María Figueres, son of Don Pepe Figueres, in a narrow victory over his PUSC opponent. His government has been faced with many of the problems of previous administrations.

A Successful Democracy

The constitution drawn up in 1949 is still the basis of government in Costa Rica. Government is divided into three branches: the executive, which consists of the president and the cabinet; the legislative, which is an assembly of representatives elected by the people; and the judicial, which includes the judges and courts. Everyone over the age of eighteen has the right to vote. Surprisingly, the constitution also abolished the army.

National Government

THE PRESIDENT IS ELECTED FOR FOUR YEARS AND CANNOT BE reelected for an immediate second term. A candidate may not be a member of the clergy and must not be related to the previous president. The successful candidate must receive at least 40 percent of the vote, otherwise a special runoff election is held between the two candidates with the most votes.

Opposite: **An election rally in a San José street**

The president is assisted by two vice presidents and a cabinet of ministers. Should the president resign or be unable to continue in office, he is succeeded by the first vice president. Next in line are the second vice president and the president of the Legislative Assembly. The cabinet consists of ministers appointed by the president. They run government ministries, which include Foreign Affairs; Public Security; Culture, Youth, and Sports; Education; and Finance.

Members of the Legislative Assembly of Costa Rica

The Legislative Assembly is made up of fifty-seven members, elected in a direct vote by the people. Deputies to the Legislative Assembly must be Costa Ricans and at least twenty-one years old. Like the president, they serve for four years and cannot be immediately reelected.

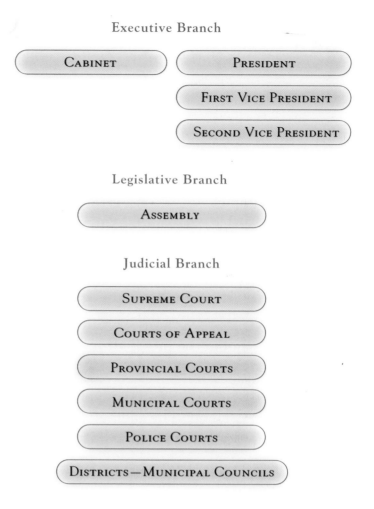

Executive Branch

CABINET   PRESIDENT

FIRST VICE PRESIDENT

SECOND VICE PRESIDENT

Legislative Branch

ASSEMBLY

Judicial Branch

SUPREME COURT

COURTS OF APPEAL

PROVINCIAL COURTS

MUNICIPAL COURTS

POLICE COURTS

DISTRICTS—MUNICIPAL COUNCILS

A unicameral (one-house) parliament, the assembly meets twice a year, although the president can convene it at other times to consider special issues. It has the power to pass laws, levy taxes, and authorize any declaration of war.

Elections for the president, the vice presidents, the Legislative Assembly, and municipal councils take place every

four years on the first Sunday in February. The elections are run by the Supreme Electoral Tribunal, which supervises the process, calls the elections, and announces the results.

Citizens line up at the polls to vote in a 1994 election.

The supreme court judges are elected by the Assembly. Judges serve for an eight-year period and are normally reelected for another eight years. Judges in the lower courts are appointed by the supreme court. Costa Rica also has criminal and civil courts.

The mounted police help patrol the plazas of San José.

A Successful Democracy **69**

The Civil Guard, which replaced the army, is responsible for enforcing law and order. Costa Rica's crime rate is relatively low, but, like other countries in Central America, illegal drugs are a serious problem.

About half the Civil Guard is stationed in San José, including the Presidential Guard. The other half works in the provinces. Also in the provinces are the town and village police. The president is the chief of all law-enforcement agencies, and there is no capital punishment in Costa Rica.

Provincial Government

Costa Rica is divided into seven provinces: San José, Alajuela, Cartago, Heredia, Guanacaste, Puntarenas, and Limón. A traveler in Costa Rica will notice that all the provinces have capitals with the same name, except Guanacaste, where the capital is Liberia.

Each province has a governor, appointed by the president. The provinces are divided into cantons, and each canton is broken up into districts. There is an elected municipal council in the chief city of each canton. Members are elected for four years and the council is responsible for all local services except police services.

Diplomatic Problems

In the 1970s, Costa Rica was drawn into the problems of Nicaragua. In 1979, when the Nicaraguan dictator Anastasio Somoza was deposed and the Sandinistas took over the government, thousands of refugees fled to Costa Rica. It was the beginning of many years of fighting with the anti-Sandinista forces (the *contra-revolutionarios*, or *contras*, meaning "those against the revolution"), who were backed by the United States and trying to regain control. Government policy, supported by the people, maintained a neutral position, which was often difficult. Eventually, in 1986,

Contra rebels train in the south of Nicaragua.

The National Flag and National Emblem

The Costa Rican national flag has five horizontal stripes of blue, white, red, white, and blue, with the red stripe twice as wide as the others. Blue is the color of the sky, white signifies peace, and red represents the cheeks of laborers.

The national emblem on the red stripe depicts three volcanic peaks, with the Caribbean Sea in the foreground and the Pacific Ocean in the background. There are also two sailing ships and seven stars representing the seven provinces.

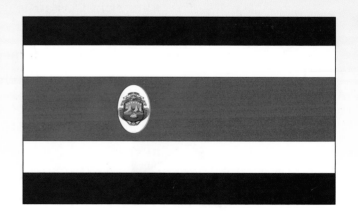

A hostage being released from the Nicaraguan Embassy in San José

President Oscar Arias Sánchez restored diplomatic relations with Nicaragua. At the same time, the government arrested and expelled contras living in Costa Rica. These actions did not please the U.S. government.

In August 1987, the presidents of El Salvador, Nicaragua, Guatemala, Honduras, and Costa Rica signed a peace agreement based on proposals presented by President Arias. In November, Costa Rica signed a border agreement with Nicaragua.

However, tensions between Costa Rica and Nicaragua resurfaced in 1993. In the Nicaraguan Embassy in San José, twenty-five people, including the ambassador, were taken hostage by armed men demanding the resignation of certain officials in Nicaragua.

In 1995, relations cooled further over Costa Rica's treatment of some illegal immigrants. Previously, Costa Rica had tolerated illegal immigrants, but now it automatically expelled them and was accused by Nicaragua of treating the immigrants violently. A month or so later, Nicaragua detained some Costa Rican Civil Guards for allegedly entering Nicaragua illegally.

Like most of its neighbors, Costa Rica receives considerable financial and technical aid from the United States. It is also dependent to some extent on the goodwill of the U.S. government in negotiating terms with North American and international banks for the loans that support the country's economy. At times, when the relationship between the two countries has been strained, the United States has cut back on the aid it gives to Costa Rica. However, since 1990 when the contra problem was largely resolved with the Sandinistas' failure to win the Nicaraguan elections, good relations between the United States and Costa Rica have been restored.

Costa Rica's National Anthem

"Noble Patria, Tu Hermosa Bandera" ("Noble Homeland, Your Beautiful Flag")
Words by José Maria Zeledón, 1900
Music by Manuel María Gutiérrez, 1853

Spanish

Noble patria, tu hermosa bandera
expresión de tu vida nos da;
bajo el límpido azul de tu cielo
blanca y pura descansa la paz.

En la lucha tenaz de fecunda labor
que enrojece del hombre la faz,
conquistaron tus hijos—labriegos
sencillos—eterno prestigio, estima y
  honor.

(repeat)

¡Salve, oh tierra gentil!
¡Salve, oh madre de amor!
Cuando alguno pretenda tu gloria
  manchar;
verás a tu pueblo valiente y viril
la tosca herramienta en arma trocar.

¡Salve, oh patria! tu pródigo suelo
dulce abrigo y sustento nos da;
bajo el límpido azul de tu cielo
¡vivan siempre el trabajo y la paz!

English Translation

Noble homeland, your beautiful flag
expresses for us your life;
under the limpid blue of your skies
peace reigns white and pure.

In the tenacious battle of fruitful toil,
that brings a glow to men's faces,
your sons—simple farmhands—
gained eternal renown, esteem and
  honor.

(repeat)

Hail, gentle country!
Hail, loving mother!
If anyone should attempt to besmirch
  your glory;
you will see your people valiant and virile
exchange their rustic tools for weapons.

Hail, oh homeland! Your prodigal soil
gives us sweet sustenance and shelter;
under the limpid blue of your sky
may peaceful labor ever continue!

A Growing Economy

Costa Rica was the first country in Central America to grow coffee. By the middle of the nineteenth century, politicians realized that the crop could be very successful. To increase production, coffee plants were given to the poor to plant wherever they could, while all homeowners were instructed to plant a few bushes and trees near their houses.

THE MESETA CENTRAL, WHERE most people were settled, proved to be an ideal location for the cultivation of coffee. It has the right altitude, with a good climate, and rich volcanic soil.

Farmers with even a modest amount of land soon found they could make an adequate, if simple, living from the plant. In the dry season, it was easy to harvest and transport the crop. Soon a constant trail of oxcarts carried coffee from the highlands to the Pacific coast. In Europe, coffee became a fashionable drink. From the 1840s onward, helped by finance and shipping from Great Britain, Costa Rica regularly exported coffee to Europe.

The climate in the Meseta Central is perfect for coffee cultivation.

What Costa Rica Grows, Makes, and Mines

Agriculture (1994)

Sugarcane	2,950,000 metric tons
Bananas	1,932,000 metric tons
Coffee	138,000 metric tons

Manufacturing (1992) *(in Costa Rican colones)*

Food products	44,484,000
Malt liquors and malt	11,172,000
Soft drinks and carbonated waters	8,978,000

Mining (1993)

Limestone	1,200,000 metric tons
Gold	19,300 troy ounces

Agriculture

Agriculture is still the foundation of Costa Rica's economy. About 28 percent of the nation's workers are connected with the agricultural industry, either working on the land or in factories processing foodstuffs. Costa Rica gets more than 60 percent of its foreign earnings from agricultural produce.

Blue bags cover growing bananas to protect the fruit from insects.

In Costa Rica, coffee and bananas continue to be important cash crops. Most of the coffee in the San José basin and in the Turrialba Valley is cultivated on a few very large coffee plantations, known as *fincas*. But many small holdings of 3.5 acres (1.4 ha) produce some of the world's highest yields per acre.

Bananas were first grown on the Caribbean coastal lowlands, but early in this century when disease threatened to destroy much of the crop, new plantations were started on the Pacific lowlands. However, as disease-resistant varieties of banana were developed, the Atlantic lowlands again became the main area of cultivation. The largest producers were the U.S.-owned Standard Fruit and United Brands companies, and bananas became the country's leading export.

A major crisis occurred in 1985 as the result of rising costs and a seventy-two-day strike (the longest in Costa Rica's history), when the Compañía Bananera de Costa Rica, a United Brands subsidiary, closed down some of its installations and laid off about 20 percent of its employees.

People were particularly hard hit in the Golfito region of the south Pacific coast. Whole towns had been completely dependent on the banana company for work. The government agreed to buy many of the abandoned plantations and buildings, with a view to cultivating cacao. In 1987, the banana industry was devastated once again when disease affected up to 80 percent of the crops.

When countries such as Costa Rica have just one or two major exports, major disasters such as hurricanes or disease can ruin the economy. Costa Rica has tried not to be so reliant on just coffee and bananas, and new cash crops include ornamental plants, cut flowers, tropical fruits, and vegetable oils.

Sugarcane has been grown as part of a scheme to produce fuel, using the fiber, or bagasse, which is left after milling. Cacao, the basis of cocoa and chocolate, is also exported, while cotton is cultivated for the textile industry. The main food crops grown for the home market are rice, corn, and beans.

Costa Rica has a growing cattle industry, which provides beef for the export market and dairy products for domestic use. The most important cattle region is Guanacaste province.

Despite its lengthy coastlines, Costa Rica has only a small fishing industry, catching mostly sardines and tuna. A shrimp industry has been started on the Pacific coast with help from foreign experts.

Costa Rican cowboys herd cattle in the hot sun.

A hydroelectric dam on the
Reventazón River

Mining and Energy

Costa Rica does not have many mineral resources. Some gold
is produced from the Santa Clara open mine, not far from San
José. Limestone and small quantities of silver, manganese, and
mercury are also mined, and there are some reserves of iron
ore and sulfur. An important discovery of bauxite has also led
to the creation of a new aluminium-smelting plant.

Almost all Costa Rica's electricity is supplied by hydro-
electricity. The three largest plants are located in the Meseta
Central. Costa Rica has some petroleum reserves, but they are
too costly to exploit, so the nation imports most of its oil. In
an effort to reduce these imports, the government has built a
geothermal power station and plans to develop some of its
coal reserves.

Coffee beans dry in the intense midday sun.

Industry

Costa Rica is more industrialized than most Central American countries. The stability of the country has allowed industry to develop and diversify. The manufacturing industry accounts for more than 20 percent of the gross national product (GNP). Factories produce many goods, and not surprisingly, in a country that is traditionally dependent on agriculture, food processing is a vital part of that industry.

The Five-Colón Note

One of the most beautiful examples of paper money in recent years is a now out-of-use five-colón note. On the reverse side, it carried a reproduction of an 1897 painting from San José's national theater by J. Villa. The painting tells the story of coffee, from harvest to export. Women picking beans are dressed in traditional colorful skirts and large straw hats. Men are carrying bags loaded with beans onto ships waiting in the harbor. And, as a reminder that Costa Rica has other crops, a man stands at the center of the painting holding a large bunch of bananas.

Fruit, meat, and vegetables are canned, and drinks such as instant coffee, beer, and spirits are produced.

Textiles are now the country's third most important export. Among the products of the chemical industry are plastics, paints, fertilizers, insecticides, and cosmetics, while other manufacturing plants produce leather items and some timber products.

Construction is also important, using mainly locally produced cement and materials. The urgent need for tourist facilities has given a great boost to the construction industry.

Ecotourism is one of Costa Rica's most lucrative industries.

Tourism

Tourism is the most recent and exciting development in Costa Rica's economy. The relatively new concept of ecotourism has encouraged thousands of foreigners to visit the country's national parks and reserves and see Costa Rica's huge diversity of plants and animals.

Other tourist features include the Irazú and Poás volcanoes, the spectacular Orosi Valley, and the ruins of the colonial church at Ujarrás, all of which can be reached easily from San José. Alternative attractions that require more travel are the Pacific beaches of Guanacaste and Puntarenas, as well as the Caribbean beaches of Limón.

Visitors enjoy the tranquillity and relative security of travel in Costa Rica, and package tours are increasing in number and size every year. A huge development known as the Papagayo Project is under way in Guanacaste province. It involves building more new hotel rooms than presently exist in all of Costa Rica.

International Trade

Today, almost half of Costa Rica's total exports go to the United States, with about 20 percent going to Europe and the remainder largely to countries in Central America. About 40 percent of Costa Rica's imports come from the United States, with Venezuela, Japan, Mexico, Guatemala, and Brazil supplying most of the balance. Costa Rica needs raw materials for industry and agriculture, consumer items, machinery and equipment, building materials, and oil.

Costa Rica is a member of the Central American Common Market. In 1994, it signed a free-trade agreement with Mexico that enables Costa Rica to sell its goods to a much larger market without controls and taxes.

Transportation

Costa Rica has easy and regular contact with the rest of the world. The main international airport, named after the drummer boy Juan Santamaría, is just outside San José. (It was previously known as Cocos International Airport.) From there, several international airlines have direct flights to North America, Europe, and Central America and, via Panama City, connections to almost anywhere in the world. A new international airport has also been built near Liberia, the capital of Guanacaste province.

End of the Line

When they were built, Costa Rica's two main railroads were vital to the country's development. The first railroad linked San José with Puerto Limón. The second line, from San José to Puntarenas, was completed in 1910. Both lines were closed, indefinitely, in 1995. For passengers, travel on these railways was slow but always interesting with frequent stops at lively platforms full of people buying and selling food and trinkets.

Lacsa, Costa Rica's national airline, has direct flights to North America and to many Central and South American cities. Lacsa and Sansa are the two major domestic airlines, and a number of other small companies make regular domestic flights. Costa Rica has other large airports at Liberia and near Puerto Limón, as well as approximately 200 smaller airfields.

Lacsa airline workers in San José

With an Atlantic coast and a Pacific coast, Costa Rica is fortunate to have several good ports that are large and modern enough for container shipping. The port of Limón and the Moín terminal on the Atlantic coast are equipped to handle the export of bananas and coffee. A new multimillion-dollar project on the Gulf of Nicoya at Caldera has now replaced Puntarenas as the main Pacific port.

The Pan-American Highway runs continuously from North America through Central America and into South America, with only a short break in Panama. There it has been impossible to build a road across the densely forested Darién region.

The first highways were built on the Meseta Central, but in recent years the government has invested heavily in roads in other parts of the country. These include new roads to Puerto Limón and the new port at Caldera.

Maintaining good roads in Costa Rica is a problem. Heavy rains, hurricanes, and the occasional earthquake cause landslides and can soon reduce a paved highway to a series of potholes. Long-distance buses are a good way to get around—reliable and inexpensive, if sometimes a little slow. The towns have buses and taxis, and rural areas have local bus service. But many people in the countryside still travel on horseback and sometimes by horse and cart.

Opposite: **Buses provide efficient transportation to city residents of San José.**

Ticos and Their Traditions

Costa Ricans are proud of their European heritage. More than 90 percent of the people are white or mestizo. Whites are descended directly from European ancestry, mainly Spanish colonists. Mestizos are people of mixed European and Native American blood. It is difficult to say what percentage of the population each represents, but the number of mestizos is increasing.

APART FROM THE ORIGINAL SPANISH SETTLERS, IMMI-grants came to Costa Rica from Germany, Great Britain, and France. More Spanish immigrants also arrived in the last century, when the coffee industry got under way. Many became successful coffee planters and exporters, merchants, ranchers, and industri-alists. Some integrated easily into society and became *Ticos,* as Costa Ricans call themselves. Others retained their national identity and traditions by establishing churches and schools in their own language.

The first few Jews, whom Costa Ricans call *polacos,* arrived from Eastern Europe in the late 1920s. Most worked in industry, commerce, and in professions such as law,

Opposite: **Stall owners are a common sight in downtown San José.**

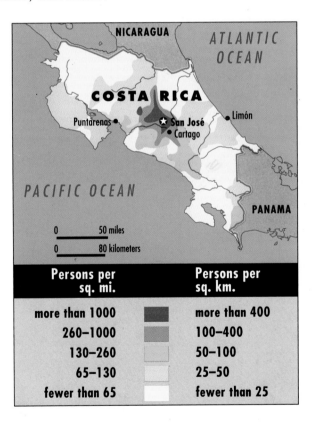

Population of Costa Rica's Largest Cities (1995)	
San José	321,193
San José (metropolitan)	959,340
Limón	56,525
Alajuela	49,115
San Isidro	41,513
Desamparados	38,858

Persons per sq. mi.		Persons per sq. km.
more than 1000		more than 400
260–1000		100–400
130–260		50–100
65–130		25–50
fewer than 65		fewer than 25

Ticos

Costa Ricans like to call themselves *Ticos*. Some say the nickname comes from an old colonial saying that "we are all *hermanticos* [little brothers]," implying equality among all the people. As if to further the idea of a united, equal society, people describe something that is very Costa Rican by saying *"es muy tico"* (es mwee TEE-ko)—"it is very Tico."

An alternative explanation is that the term may simply reflect the common use of the diminutive ending *-tico*, which in Spanish means "little" or "small." Costa Ricans tend to use *-tico* and *-ico* at the end of words such as *momentico,* meaning "just a little moment." In other Spanish-speaking countries, people are more likely to say *"momentito,"* which is the correct word in Spanish.

Costa Ricans also like to call one another by nicknames. Someone who is fat may be called *gordo* (GOR-doh) and a thin person *flaco* (FLA-koh), but no offense is meant—or taken. A common expression that everyone uses to friends and strangers is *mi amor* (MEE a-MOR), meaning "my love." It has no deep significance, just that the Costa Ricans like to be warm and friendly.

They are also very polite. On being introduced to another person, the Costa Rican greeting is *"con mucho gusto"* (kohn MOO-choh GOO-stoh), which means "with much pleasure." This may be followed at the end of the conversation by *"para servirle"* (PAH-ra sayr-VEER-lay), meaning "at your service," or *"que le vaya bien"* (kay lay VAH-ya BEE-en), meaning "may you go well."

medicine, and accounting. Recently, they have entered politics, and more are working in government.

But a familiar sight in parts of Costa Rica are polacos who make a living as traveling salespeople. They sell all sorts of goods from clothes to household items, and they can be paid in weekly installments. Other Costa Ricans have joined in this form of commercial activity, which is now an important part of the country's economy.

In the urban areas, many people work as civil servants for the government, while others enjoy various professional careers. Restaurants, hotels, shopping centers, and supermarkets employ a high percentage of the population, and about the same number work in manufacturing industries. Women do all these jobs, too, but they are generally outnumbered by men. However, more women work in community and social services.

A familiar sight in downtown San José are the many fruit and vegetable stands, owned by both men and women. Outside the towns, most villages and communities on the Meseta Central are involved in the coffee, sugarcane, and dairy industries.

Costa Rica's abundant produce is sold both locally and around the world.

Who Lives in Costa Rica?	
Whites	87%
Mestizos	7%
Blacks	3%
East Asians (mostly Chinese)	2%
Native Americans	1%

The largest minority group in Costa Rica is made up of the blacks of the Caribbean coast. They are descendants of the West Indians who arrived, mainly from Jamaica, to help build the Atlantic railroad and who subsequently stayed to work on the banana plantations. As English-speaking and British subjects, the West Indians had a very different culture from that of the Ticos, who initially wanted nothing to do with them.

But in the 1920s, when employment in the highlands became difficult and it was obvious that things were going well on the banana plantations, many Ticos moved to the coast. This led to friction as the Ticos soon came to resent the status of the English-speaking blacks and the higher wages they received.

In the 1930s, when disease devastated the Caribbean banana plantations, the United Fruit Company transferred its operations to the Pacific coast. They were subsequently forbidden by law to take the "coloreds" with them. Many blacks then went to Panama and the United States to look for work, especially during World War II.

Others stayed on the Caribbean coast and made a living as best they could by clearing and farming small plots

A black barber in Limón

of land in the forest. However, when this first generation of blacks produced families, the children were not accepted by the Costa Rican government either as British subjects or as Costa Ricans.

It was not until 1948, after the revolution in which many blacks supported Figueres's cause, that a decree was passed ensuring that every person born in Costa Rica had all the rights of Costa Rican citizenship.

The Brown Province

Nearly one-fifth of the population lives in the Pacific northwest region. This is sometimes called the "brown" province because of the mixture of people of Spanish, Indian, and African origins. Those of African origin are descendants of slaves brought to Costa Rica in the seventeenth and eighteenth centuries. Many people in this region work on large ranches, or *haciendas*. Others cultivate their own small farms. The cowboys, known as *sabañeros*, were once seen as romantic figures—tough and lonely, herding cattle day and night on the vast plains. Today, they are just as tough and hardworking, but much of the romance has gone.

Educated blacks now work in many professions, while in Limón province, where they make up about one-third of the population, most are independent cacao farmers or workers on the banana plantations.

Native Americans

Only a very small number of Native American peoples, between 5,000 and 10,000, have survived in Costa Rica, and today their lifestyle is little different from that of ordinary, poor *campesinos*, or rural people. Most live in the south of the country.

The largest group are the Bribrí and Cabecar peoples. Some live on a reserve set aside for them by the government in an isolated region of the Cordillera de Talamanca. The second-largest group are the Boruca, of whom fewer than 2,000 have survived. Most speak Spanish, and they have substantial contact with other Costa Ricans and occasional tourists, as their reserve is not far from a main highway. Tourists like to watch the Boruca craftworkers. The women make clothes and bags on homemade looms, and the men make masks of balsa wood.

Chorotegas

The Chorotega lived in Guanacaste province and were probably the most important group of Native Americans at the time of the Spanish conquest. They may have come from Mexico around A.D. 800. Influenced by the well-developed Mayan peoples of Mexico and Guatemala, they are best remembered today for their pottery. In the small town of Guaitíl, on the site of an ancient Chorotega community, some women set up a workshop twenty years ago to produce Chorotega-style pots. They use traditional methods and materials to re-create the striking black, red, and white patterns or animal motifs found on ancient Chorotega pottery.

Bribrí girls making
sandwiches for lunch

For many years, Costa Rican society ignored the Native
American peoples. In the 1960s, following a newspaper campaign
highlighting their problems, a National Commission of Indian
Affairs was created. Its aim was to improve the education, health,
nutrition, and community life of this small group of people.

Today, most Native American families live simply, in
houses of palm thatch and bamboo. Near their homes, they
cultivate a variety of crops, including bananas, corn, beans,

and fruit, but they do not own the land on which they live, and they are constantly under threat from speculators. (Speculators are people who want to take over land so they can profit from it, perhaps by planting crops or raising cattle.) And, as the tourist industry develops, speculators are also looking for sites where they can build hotels and other tourist facilities.

In 1994, the Bribrí and Cabecar peoples took a major step forward in running their own affairs. In the past, native peoples have had problems trying to raise funds from ordinary banks. So with the help of the Inter-American Development Bank, they founded their own bank. Now at least they have a chance of buying their own land or starting up a business.

Language

Spanish is Costa Rica's official language. Compared with the language of other Spanish-speaking countries, Costa Rican Spanish is quite formal. People speak distinctly, slowly, and without dropping letters at the ends of words. An example of their formality is the use of the word *usted* when speaking to children. Usually in Spanish, children are addressed as *tu*, which is familiar and friendly. In other countries, *usted* is reserved for people one does not know well or for someone who is greatly respected.

Tiquismos

Some slang words and expressions have crept into Costa Rican Spanish, which the *Ticos* refer to as *tiquismos*, though several of the words are used in other countries also.

For example:

¡achará! (ach-a-RAH)	What a pity!
buena nota (BWAYN-a-NOH-ta)	how cool, great (good note)
¿diay? (dee-AH-ee)	Oh dear, but what can you expect?
maje (MAH-hay)	buddy, pal, or mate (used by young men)
pura vida (POO-rah VEE-dah)	great, okay, cool (pure life)

Spanish is the official language of Costa Rica.

Perhaps even more difficult for a foreigner to grasp is the Costa Rican use of *vos*. It is another way of saying "you," but it is very old-fashioned. Any sentence using *vos* must also have the correct verb ending to follow it. So "you want" becomes *vos queréis*, rather than the better known (and easier) *tu quieres* or *usted quiere*.

English, the second most common language, is now taught in all public schools. A few black communities on the Caribbean coast, descendants of English-speaking West Indians, speak a form of pidgin English.

Most Native American languages have died out. However, in the Talamanca region, some local radio programs and newspaper articles are produced in Bribrí. The University of Costa Rica has also published a grammar and spelling book in Bribrí, which it is hoped will help the language to survive.

Other Immigrants

English is taught as a second language in public schools throughout Costa Rica.

People of Chinese ancestry have also settled in Costa Rica. Some are descendants of workers brought in to help on the railroad to the Caribbean coast, but others arrived during this

century. In San José, the Chinese, or *chinos*, as they are known locally, have been absorbed easily into the urban lifestyle. But in smaller towns, especially in the lowlands, they are more conspicuous because they own many of the retail shops, restaurants, and movie theaters. They also work as traders in the cacao and banana industries.

The most recent and largest group of people to arrive in Costa Rica are the tens of thousands of refugees from other parts of Central America. Their arrival has put a great strain on the country's health, educational, and social-welfare facilities.

Perhaps the greatest cultural change has occurred, however, because of the many U.S. and Canadian citizens who have taken up temporary or permanent residence in Costa Rica. These include diplomats, businesspeople, missionaries, and Peace Corps volunteers, as well as older citizens who have decided to retire there. In just a few years, signs for U.S.-style fast food have appeared all over San José, and tourist police in uniforms similar to those worn by Canadian Mounties patrol the streets on horseback.

A Nation of Faith

Roman Catholicism was first introduced in Costa Rica by Spanish missionaries in the sixteenth century. It is now the official religion, and nine out of ten Ticos call themselves Catholics. Few, however, are regular churchgoers, though they do believe strongly in the power of Catholic saints.

AFTER INDEPENDENCE, THE CHURCH BECAME A POWERFUL organization involved in education and some state affairs. This power was reduced in the 1880s when the government decided to separate the affairs of the church from those of the state. It also abolished religious teaching in public schools and allowed people to divorce.

The 1949 constitution provides that the state contribute to the upkeep of the Catholic Church. At the same time, it recognizes that everyone has the freedom to practice the religion of his or her choice.

Today, religion is again part of the school curriculum, and religious celebrations continue to play an important part in

Native Beliefs

It was not easy for the Spanish missionaries to convert the Native Americans to Christianity. The tribes had their own beliefs, which revolved around their creator god and spirits who existed in the natural world in which they lived. In their spiritual world, the Bribrí and Cabecar believed the forest was created by Sibö, their creator god. The ceiba, or silk cotton tree, they recognized as the mother of Tbekol, the Big Snake. The early tribes also had shamans and sorcerers whose work was to cure the sick, prophesy the future, and placate evil spirits.

Opposite: **A church sits in the shadow of Arenal Volcano.**

Religions of Costa Rica

Roman Catholic	80%
Evangelical Protestant	15%
Other	5%

Evangelical Protestants are a small minority of Costa Rica's population.

Costa Rican family and community life. Baptism is one of the most important family occasions, along with a child's first communion, and a church wedding.

Many villages and towns are named after saints, and the patron saint's day is still widely celebrated. Also, most homes, offices, and schools have a crucifix, shrine, or some kind of religious poster on the wall.

While the church is not officially permitted to be involved in politics, it is concerned with social conditions. Nuns and priests work among the poor, nursing and caring but also helping to teach skills and crafts that might help families to improve their way of life.

Some private high schools are run by Catholic priests and nuns, and the church exerts considerable influence through sermons and religious instruction.

Churches

Among the fine churches in Costa Rica are the Metropolitan Cathedral in San José and, not far from the capital, the impressive Gothic-style Church of San Isidro de Coronado. Cartago has the huge *Basilica de Nuestra Señora de Los Angeles* (Our Lady of the Angels), Costa Rica's most famous church, while Ujarrás in the beautiful Orosi Valley has one of the very few remaining colonial

churches. The Church of Our Lady of the Immaculate
Conception, now mostly in ruins, was built in 1693 and
destroyed in 1833 by floods.

The Basilica de Nuestra Señora de Los Angeles in Cartago

Minority Religions

A minority of the Costa Rican people belong to Protestant
churches. Traditionally, most are from the West Indian families of the Caribbean coast, but their numbers are increasing
in the Meseta Central, particularly with the arrival of evangelical missionaries from the United States and elsewhere.
These include groups such as the Assemblies of God and
Jehovah's Witnesses.

Christmas

Although Costa Ricans are not a strongly religious people, they do celebrate religious holidays, such as Christmas and Easter. Christmas in Costa Rica is celebrated in much the same way as it is in Europe and the United States. Preparation starts weeks beforehand with decorated Christmas trees, colored lights, shops filled with toys, and a huge assortment of other gifts. Santa Claus is traditional, dressed in his red suit with white fur trim and big boots, and sporting a bushy, long white beard. In San José during Christmas week, fireworks, bullfights, and fun fairs add to the excitement.

Indoors, families make their own crèche scenes, though it is not until Christmas Eve that the Christ child is laid in the manger. On Christmas Eve, families and friends gather to eat turkey and corn tamales and to drink well, though the children are usually eager to get to bed, anticipating what Santa Claus will bring. Many families continue with the festivities until the New Year.

A resplendent Easter procession on the Nicoya Peninsula

Saints' Days

Some of the most important festivals in Costa Rica are saints' days. Festivals are held in towns and villages throughout the country in honor of their patron saints. Carrying a statue of the saint through the streets of the city, town, or village is a traditional part of saints' day festivities. Once the religious part of the ceremony is over, everyone joins in the dancing. Sometimes there are rodeos or bullfights and, almost always, fireworks.

Our Lady of the Angels

The most important festival is the Feast of Our Lady of the Angels on August 2, which celebrates the patron saint of Costa Rica. Every year, thousands of pilgrims make their way to the Basilica de Nuestra Señora de Los Angeles in Cartago. The basilica is built on the spot where on August 2, 1635, the Virgin is said to have appeared, in the form of a black stone doll, to a poor peasant girl. The story goes that every time the girl took the doll away with her, it reappeared on the same spot. Local people interpreted this as a sign and built the basilica.

A black stone image of the Virgin Mary, known as La Negrita and no more than 6 inches (15 cm) high, is kept in a special chapel in the basilica. Pilgrims approach the statue on their knees, and on August 2, they parade it in a colorful procession from the basilica to other churches in the city.

The First Protestants

Captain William Le Lacheur, the merchant who took the first cargo of coffee beans to England, was probably the first to distribute Bibles in Costa Rica. With his son John and his friend Dr. Richard Brealey, he began the first Protestant services in the country. Dr. Brealey, the first lay pastor, held services in his home for seventeen years.

In 1864, the Protestant community decided to have its own church, and in 1865 a prefabricated, iron-structured church was brought from England on one of Le Lacheur's ships. The Church of the Good Shepherd was erected in San José, and plaques in the church commemorate the work of both men in establishing the Protestant faith in Costa Rica.

The golden altar of the Basilica de Nuestra Señora de Los Angles

Culture, the Arts, and Recreation

A quick glance at a list of national holidays in Costa Rica reveals that there is one holiday almost every month—and sometimes two. For important holidays such as Easter and Christmas, the whole country shuts down. Banks, post offices, museums, and government offices close, usually for an entire week.

DIFFERENT PEOPLE CELEBRATE THE HOLIDAYS IN DIFFERENT ways. For many, the holidays provide a chance to get away from the city and spend the time quietly in the countryside, walking or hiking in the mountains, or simply relaxing on the beach. Costa Ricans have an extraordinary choice of beautiful places to go, and they make the most of it.

Religious festivals are quite common in Costa Rica.

Even for a local festival in the provinces, everything shuts down for several days. This is particularly the case in Guanacaste for the celebration on July 25 of their independence from Nicaragua in 1824. The same is true in Limón on October 12 when El Día de la Raza (Columbus Day) is celebrated.

Columbus Day in Limón

While *Carnaval* is celebrated everywhere else in Central America just before Lent, it takes place in Limón during the week before Columbus Day, the anniversary of the day Columbus arrived in the Americas. The idea caught on after Arthur King, a local man, reported what he had seen of cele-

Opposite: **A young girl walks in costume during an Easter procession.**

Festival of the Devils

A fiesta that takes place in many parts of Central and South America mimics the conquest of the invading Spaniards over the Native Indians. In Costa Rica, it has survived among the Boruca peoples who celebrate the *Fiesta de los Diablitos*, meaning "Celebration of the little Devils," for three days over the New Year.

A man from the village plays the part of a bull—representing the Spaniards—and other villagers become "devils." They disguise themselves with homemade balsawood masks. At midnight on December 30, the devils meet on the top of a hill with local musicians playing pipes, drums, and guitars. During that night and for the next three days, they taunt the "bull," while moving from house to house to receive food and drink. Eventually the bull is killed, and contrary to historical fact, the Indians are seen as the conquerors of the Spaniards.

brations for Columbus Day when he was working in the Panama Canal Zone. At Carnaval time, Limón is packed with Costa Ricans from every part of the country, as well as international tourists. Most spectacular is the *Grand Desfile*, a parade of floats with people dressed in brilliant African-Caribbean costumes. Other events include music festivals, theater, bull running, and dazzling displays of fireworks.

But the heart of Carnaval is the music. Limón throbs to the sound of every kind of African-Caribbean beat, played on tambourines, drums, and whistles. Every corner of the town seems to be alive with discos, live bands, and blasting sound systems, though most of the action is actually centered on an area around the port. There, people dance the night away.

Fairs

Towns and villages throughout Costa Rica hold their own fairs, which are opportunities for the whole community to get together and have some fun. Entertainment includes fun-fair

Weddings

Weddings in Costa Rica are like those in the United States and Europe. Most people get married in a church with a religious service. The bride's family are hosts for the occasion, with parties sometimes both before and after the wedding. Everyone drinks, dances, and has a good time. The evening ends with a meal. The newlyweds leave for their honeymoon, while everyone else goes home.

rides, bingo, and bullfighting. There are beauty contests, firework displays, bands, dancing, and stalls piled high with food and drink.

Music

When President Don Pepe Figueres created the Ministry of Culture, Youth, and Sports in 1970, it gave a new impetus to the arts, and especially to music.

Special attention was given to the National Symphony Orchestra, which before 1970 presented just a few concerts

Opposite: **Fairs draw crowds of people, and sometimes animals, for the festivities.**

each year. Under the guidance of American Peace Corps worker Gerald Brown, the orchestra was revitalized. Other foreigners were also invited to teach the use of instruments and to conduct. In 1978, the orchestra performed at the White House in Washington, D.C., and at the United Nations headquarters in New York City.

Costa Rica also has a state-funded Youth Symphony Orchestra. Prominent composers include Julio Fonseca Gutiérrez and Julio Mata Oreamuno, who is perhaps best known for *Suite Abstracta* and the operetta *Toyupán*.

The Castella Conservatory and the National Dance Company are two of the main venues for productions in San José. The National Theatre is also in the capital, and theater groups are attached to both the University of Costa Rica and the National University.

Dance

Few traditional folk dances have survived in Costa Rica, but the best come from Guanacaste province. The most popular is the lively and colorful Punto Guanacaste dance, backed by the music of the guitar and a kind of xylophone called the marimba.

On the Caribbean coast, traditional dances are part of the maypole festival. Colored ribbons are tied to the top of a pole, and in the dance style known as a quadrille, dancers weave in and out, so that the ribbons fold over one another down the length of the pole. Other folk traditions are also expressed in dances of the colonial era, such as waltzes, *pasillos*, and mazurkas, which folk groups perform in period costume.

The Saturday dance at the local dance hall is a popular night out, especially for young Costa Ricans. With tremendous energy, they dance for hours to Latin music, such as the salsa and lambada, as well as to Caribbean rhythms. They also enjoy rock and swing music from North America and a variety of hits from Europe.

Art

The earliest known forms of art in Costa Rica are the fine jade, gold, and ceramic artifacts that were found in the graves of ancient civilizations. They can be seen in the country's museums.

The Jade Museum

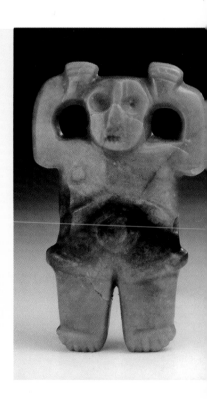

In an ordinary-looking office building in downtown San José, on the eleventh floor, is the *Marco Fidel Tristan Museo de Jade*, or the Jade Museum. The exterior of the building may not look like much, but it holds the world's largest collection of American jade.

A staggering number of jade artifacts carved and sculpted by early civilizations are on display. Most experts assume that the jade was brought in from present-day Guatemala, as there are no known sources of it in Costa Rica.

Among the jade objects are axe-gods, pendants in the shape of an ax, with the carved upper part depicting a freakish human or animal. The animal figures resemble jaguars or cats, monkeys, birds, reptiles, and a double-headed crocodile. There are also decorative objects such as nose rings.

Gold artifacts include some that were used as decoration, such as neck bands, headbands, and earrings, as well as more functional objects such as breastplates. Ceramics range over a period from about 300 B.C. to A.D. 1550 and include the three-legged *metate* tables used for grinding maize. There are also pottery bowls, jars, and figurines, many intricately decorated with motifs of animals and weird human faces of mythical and spiritual significance.

The folk art most closely associated with Costa Rica are the gaily painted oxcarts once used by country people to take their produce to market. The wife of a rural cart maker is thought to have been the first to make the stylized designs of flowers, leaves, and vegetables. Today, the carts are a feature in local festivals and are sold in miniature for the tourist market. Other crafts include mahogany wood bowls and trays, woven baskets and mats, and many leather goods.

Painted oxcarts *(right and below)* **are familiar examples of folk art in Costa Rica.**

Francisco Amighetti Ruis

Costa Rica does not have a strong tradition in painting, sculpture, or folk arts. Best known is the work of engraver, graphic artist, and painter Francisco Amighetti Ruis, born in 1907, the son of an Italian immigrant. Many of his wood engravings and paintings depict contemporary people and customs of Costa Rica, but he also traveled a great deal in Mexico and South and Central America, and influences from these places appear in his work.

Ruis introduced mural painting to Costa Rica and wrote several books containing accounts of his travels. Since the 1960s, the government has given more support to the arts, and young contemporary artists are now experimenting with new ideas and materials. Among them are Celia Lacayo, Johnny Villares, and Isidro Con Wong.

Literature

Writers of the twentieth century have concentrated largely on the political and social scene around them. One of the most respected, Joaquín García Monge, wrote the first important Costa Rican novel, *El Moto*. Also, from 1919 to 1958, he edited *El Repertorio Americano*, a magazine widely acclaimed for its intellectual and literary essays.

Among his contemporaries were Roberto Brenes Mesén and Ricardo Fernández Guardia, both highly regarded for their works on education and history. In the 1930s and 1940s, many writings concerned the exploitation of peasants by landlords. *Mamita Yunái*, written by Carlos Luis Fallas about the plight of the banana workers, is one of the best.

Another writer who explores a similar theme of social protest is Fabián Dobles. His novels, *Ese que Llaman Pueblo* and *El Sitio de las Abras*, have been well received internationally.

Costa Ricans are passionate about soccer, or *fútbol*, the national sport. During the season, matches are played regularly in San José's Saprissa Stadium in front of large crowds of enthusiastic spectators. From an early age, young children kick a ball around on any spare patch of ground, and adults do much the same when they are not working.

Other sports enjoyed in Costa Rica include basketball, volleyball, baseball, and tennis; golf and polo are enjoyed by the wealthy, while pool is also popular. The Meseta Central is good country for horseback riding. As if all this were not enough, Costa Rica is a marvelous place for water sports. There is excellent sea fishing, and for many, the uncrowded

Soccer is a passion for many Costa Ricans.

beaches that are safe for swimming offer the best opportunity to relax.

Good surfing is only a few hours from anywhere in Costa Rica, which has some of the best surfing waves in the world. Internationally, Lake Arenal is recognized as one of the best places for windsurfing, with good, steady winds from December to April, but the coast also has places to windsurf, and to scuba dive among schools of exotic fish and beautiful corals.

White-water rafting and kayaking are the newest and most popular sports in the country. The excellent conditions on some of Costa Rica's rivers have already attracted international competitors and many tourists.

A kayaker off the coast of Montezuma

Living and Learning

More than half of Costa Rica's people live on the Meseta Central, while very few live in the large tracts of lowlands on the Caribbean coast. Although the population is not evenly distributed, about the same number of Costa Ricans live in the countryside as live in the towns. In the world today, this is quite unusual.

IN MOST DEVELOPING COUNTRIES MANY PEOPLE MOVE FROM rural areas into towns and cities seeking better economic opportunities. Costa Ricans will tell you that they remain in rural areas because their roots are in the land. In many ways, family life is more important to Costa Ricans than the benefits of relocation. Family loyalty is strong, and in rural areas, families help one another in the house and on the farms.

Towns, of course, can offer much more than the countryside in terms of education, hospitals and clinics, and entertainment. And some people have taken their chances and set up a home, often illegally, on the outskirts of San José or some other cities.

A concrete block house in the Meseta Central

Traditionally in Costa Rica, the father is head of the household, and the mother takes care of family and household matters. Boys are not expected to do "girls' work" and are given more freedom. Girls have always lived a more sheltered life. But times are changing. Women now have a much more active life in work outside the home.

Opposite: **A house near Cartago**

National Holidays in Costa Rica

New Year's Day	January 1
St. Joseph's Day	March 19
Ash Wednesday	Wednesday before Lent begins
Holy Week	Week before Easter
Juan Santamaría Day	April 11
Labor Day	May 1
Feast of Our Lady of the Angels	August 2
Feast of the Assumption and Mother's Day	August 15
Independence Day	September 15
Columbus Day	October 12
All Souls' Day	November 2
Christmas Day	December 25

Children must attend school until age fifteen.

Education

As early as 1869, Costa Rican law decreed that all children must attend school and that schooling should be free.

Between 1885 and 1888, Minister of Education Mauro Fernández opened many schools, provided textbooks, and insisted on establishing qualification requirements for teachers. Large sums of money from the coffee industry helped him succeed. In about thirty years, the number of people who could not read or write dropped from about 75 to 25 percent of the population.

Education in Costa Rica accounts for 20 to 25 percent of the national budget. About one of every four civil servants is a teacher.

By law, the government must provide a school in every canton and in every population center with more than 5,000 residents. In earlier days, many people in rural areas helped to build their own schools and, where there were no schools, the municipal councils paid bus fares for children to get to the nearest high school.

Espaleta

Children in Costa Rica learn to ride horses at a very early age. In rural areas, it is still one of the best ways of getting around. One popular game—*espaleta*—requires excellent horsemanship. It is regularly played at village fairs and also between groups of men and boys just for fun. In *espaleta*, each competitor races on horseback down a length of track or path at great speed, holding a small metal lance. The object of the game is to stick the lance through a ring that is suspended from a rope at the end of the path. The problem is that the ring is only slightly larger than a wedding ring. The winner is the person who passes the lance through the ring most times.

Going to School

Costa Rican children are expected to go to school from the age of six until they are at least fifteen years old. They spend six years at primary level; the secondary level is a basic three-year course. Students may then concentrate on just two or three subjects for another two years before deciding whether to attend a university or college.

Subjects studied include Spanish and English, social studies, mathematics, sciences, music, religion, arts and technology (such as photography), physical education, and theater studies. The school year begins in March and ends in November, with a two-week holiday in July.

The University of Costa Rica was established in 1940, with departments of law, fine arts, agriculture, pharmacy, and education. Other departments, such as dentistry and journalism, have since been added to cope with modern demands.

The computer lab at the University of Costa Rica

In the 1970s, because so many more students wanted a higher education, the National University in Heredia, the Costa Rica Technological Institute, and several regional university centers were built. A number of students also attend university courses overseas, particularly in the United States, while Costa Rican universities attract students from other parts of Central America.

In 1976, the Central American Autonomous University was opened as a private institute and has gained a reputation for its academic excellence. The State University at a Distance—a form of open university—founded in 1978, offers courses by radio and television.

The Central American Institute for Business Administration was founded in 1964 with the technical help of Harvard University's graduate school of business and financial support from the U.S. government.

Literacy and Libraries

As education has become widespread, the number of adults able to read and write has increased to more than 90 percent of the population.

To support the educational system, Costa Rica has many libraries. The National Library in San José has an extensive and varied range of many fine works. There are also libraries in all the universities and institutes of higher education and in

Carmen Naranjo

Carmen Naranjo is one of Costa Rica's most remarkable women. Her novels and short-story collections have been widely translated, and she has received a number of literary awards. She has combined her work, as one of the country's most successful writers, with a number of high-profile public offices—including secretary of culture, director of the publishing house EDUCA, and ambassador to Israel.

the secondary schools, as well as public libraries in the capitals and villages of the cantons, and rural libraries. Because of the increasing number of publishing houses in Costa Rica, many more books are now produced locally.

The entrance to the National Library in San José

Newspapers and Television

Costa Rica enjoys freedom of the press. Because most people speak Spanish and almost everyone is literate, there is a wide readership for newspapers and magazines.

Most of the newspapers, magazines, publishing houses, and radio and TV stations are based in San José. The three major daily newspapers, all tabloids, are *La Nación, La República,* and *La Prensa Libre.* The *Tico Times* is published weekly in English.

The majority of articles and stories are about events in Costa Rica, though some international news is included. Many pages cover sports matches and results, and there is usually a page devoted to local crimes and accidents.

A newspaper stand in San José

Magazines published for women are very popular, with features on fashion, domestic issues, and romance.

About 98 percent of Costa Ricans have radios, and television networks cover 90 percent of the country. There are several religious and cultural networks.

Mexican and North American films are relayed, and live TV from the United States is received by satellite and cable. However, "imported culture" is not universally popular, and many people would like to see more programs produced locally.

Housing

Houses, and the materials used to build them, depend on the location in Costa Rica. On the Meseta Central, most working people live in houses built of concrete blocks or bricks with tile or corrugated iron roofs. Many are one-story houses, and most are painted in bright colors.

A poor barrio north of the center of San José

Inside, the main room is the *sala*, where guests are entertained. It is usually furnished with a couch and chairs, a central table, and several pictures or posters on the walls. The other rooms in the house are the kitchen, maybe a dining room, a bathroom, and two or three bedrooms.

Older houses on the Meseta Central, and those in remote regions, are built in adobe mud brick with a roof of clay tiles. Some have verandas overlooking central patios. In rural areas, porches and roofs are often covered with flowers, ferns, and other greenery.

Although most houses have running water and electricity, the exceptions are the ramshackle dwellings on the outskirts of San José and other towns. Made of wood, cardboard, corrugated iron, or whatever other materials are available, these homes are very basic.

At the other extreme, wealthy people have impressive houses, often surrounded by a high concrete wall to deter intruders. These houses are similar to houses in the United States or Europe, with garages, carports, paved driveways,

and maybe swimming pools and recreation rooms.

Homes in the coastal lowlands are generally built of wood and stand on stilts as protection against flooding and animals. The shaded space under the floor can be used as a work area and for drying clothes. Many have shutters rather than windows to let air circulate and balconies where families and friends can sit and chat in the warm evenings.

Stilted houses protect homeowners from floods and animals.

Health

Good health is closely associated with a clean water supply and nutritious food, and in recent years, the Costa Rican government has worked hard to improve both. Now, 94 percent of the people have access to safe water.

The government has also taken steps to reduce malnutrition. Not having enough of the right kind of food was for many years a main reason why so many children died young. In 1970, a program of rural health was begun to provide two meals a day for primary-school and preschool children, as well as for pregnant women and nursing mothers.

Another benefit of the program was the establishment of medical posts that

A Growing Population

Costa Rica's population is growing at an annual rate of 2.1 percent, above average in Central American countries. As early as the 1960s, doctors were advising on birth control, which has helped slow the birthrate. But if it continues at the present rate, Costa Rica's population will double in thirty-five years.

doctors and nurses would visit on a regular basis, especially in small rural communities. Vaccinations, medicines, and health care for pregnant mothers were provided in the attempt to cut down disease. Even so, dysentery and typhoid are still a problem in some areas.

There is approximately one doctor for every one thousand people, but the best hospitals and medical treatment are in San José. Medical schools train new doctors, and part of their training is spent working in rural areas. However, many people still have great faith in herbal medicines, and stands of dried plants and herbs can be found in many markets.

Social Welfare

Costa Rica has one of the best social welfare programs in Central America, but it will be under even greater pressure if its population continues to increase at the current rate. At present, the welfare system uses up almost 45 percent of the national budget.

The national government began a vaccination campaign in October 1997.

Social welfare provides a complete program of care and assistance for workers and their families. This includes financial help for employed people who suffer an injury, for the sick, and for pregnant women who are on maternity leave. Workers are also entitled to old-age pensions, and the disabled receive help as well.

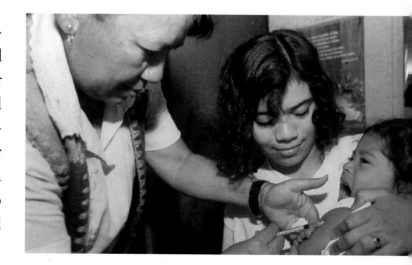

Food

Sitting down to breakfast, a typical Costa Rican family is likely to be eating *gallo pinto*, which many people regard as the country's national dish. *Gallo pinto* means "painted rooster," but the name has little relation to the dish, which is made of red and white beans, white rice, onions, peppers, and seasonings. Sometimes it is served with scrambled eggs. The intention behind such a big breakfast, it seems, is to go out and work it off. Of course, in rural areas this is exactly what people do.

Beans and rice are the basics of many Costa Rican dishes. Perhaps the best known is *casado* (married person), a dish in which stewed beef or fish, fried plantains, cabbage, or coleslaw are added to rice and beans.

Many dishes are prepared as soups and stews, such as *olla de carne*. Also known as *la olla* (the kettle), it consists of beef, plantain, corn, yucca, *ñampi*, and chayote, which are local

Mounds of fresh bread await customers at a bakery in San José.

vegetables. Other favorites are *sopa negra*—black beans with a poached egg—and *picadillo*, a meat and vegetable stew.

Although Costa Rica has two long coastlines, most people prefer to eat red meat rather than fish. The exception is a dish called *ceviche*, which consists of raw fish marinated in lime juice with onion, garlic, and coriander.

Tortillas are often eaten with a main meal, but they are also filled with meat or cheese to serve as a snack. Other snacks include *arreglados*, made from bread, meat, and vegetables; and empanadas, small pastry pies with similar fillings. *Pan de yuca*, or yucca bread, is a specialty sold in street markets.

Caribbean Cooking

Many Costa Ricans in the highlands cook on woodstoves, and in the Caribbean region, most still use wood fires.

Caribbean, or Creole, cooking is different from highland cuisine in that it uses many more spices, such as coriander, cumin, paprika, cloves, and chilies. The other secret is coconut milk, which can turn a fairly average dish of rice and beans into a delicious meal. Coconut milk is also the vital ingredient in "rundown," which sounds like "rondon" in the local dialect. Rundown is a vegetable stew made with meat or fish, plantains, and breadfruit. The best rundown is cooked for many hours.

Costa Ricans love sweet puddings and cakes, and a favorite in the Caribbean lowlands is *pan bon*, a sweet, sticky bun glazed with cheese and fruit.

A Feast of Fruits

Many different kinds of fruit are grown in Costa Rica, including bananas, pineapples, papayas *(above)*, mangoes, passion fruits, melons, and lemons. Less familiar fruits include:

pejbayes—small green or orange palm fruits widely used in cooking. They are related to the coconut.

mamones chinos—small red or yellow fruits with a spiny skin and fleshy fruit. Often sold by the dozen on street corners.

anona—custard apple. Fruit with the taste of custard.

carambolá—star apple. When the fruit is cut, it has the shape of a star.

marañón—its seed is the cashew nut.

guanábana (left)—soursop, mainly from the Caribbean region.

tamarindo—fruit of the tamarind tree. The sticky pulp that surrounds seeds in large pods is used as a flavoring, particularly in drinks.

Guanacaste Gourmet

Guanacaste cooking is distinctive in its use of corn, the crop most widely grown by the Chorotega, the original Native Americans of this region.

Corn is the basis of tortillas, the thin floury pancakes eaten almost everywhere in Central America and Mexico. Usually they are filled with meat, chicken, or cheese. *Chorreados*, another kind of pancake, are generally served with *natilla*, which is rather like sour cream. Tamales, which were known to the Chorotega, are still a favorite festival food. They are made from corn dough, with a variety of fillings, wrapped in banana leaves, and boiled.

In Guanacaste, anyone looking for a quick snack that can be bought from a roadside stand should try the sconelike *tanelas* or *rosquillas*. One traveler described them as tasting like a combination of tortillas and doughnuts! Favorite corn-based drinks include *horchata*, which is spiced with cinnamon, and *pinolillo*, made with roasted corn.

The most popular drink is, of course, coffee. It is now more than 150 years since the crop was first imported from Cuba or Jamaica and cultivated in the Central Valley. For many years, it was Costa Rica's major export. In the late nineteenth century, it brought hope and prosperity to a society that 100 years earlier was the poorest in Central America. Coffee has funded much of the country's development—its roads, bridges, schools, hospitals, railroads, and many public buildings. And coffee landlords have become presidents! Costa Rica's high-quality coffee has earned its name: *grano d'oro*—the golden bean.

A woman quietly enjoys a hot cup of coffee.

Timeline

Costa Rica's History

World History

Costa Rica's History

Mexico, Costa Rica, and other Central American territories gain independence from Spain.	1821
The Central American territories leave the Mexican Empire and form the United Provinces of Central America.	1823
Dissolution of the United Provinces of Central America.	1838
Costa Rica joins Nicaragua to defeat William Walker.	1855
General Tomás Guardia overthrows the government of Costa Rica.	1870
José Joaquín Rodríguez elected president in first democratic elections in Central America.	1890
Rafael Angel Caldéron Guardia of the National Republican Party (PRN) wins the election and begins to institute social reforms.	1940
Jose Figueres Ferrer leads effort to seat elected president Otilio Ulate Blanco and end civil war.	1948
The volcano Irazú erupts and showers tons of ash over San José and much of the surrounding countryside.	1963 – 1965
Several political parties join together to form the Social Christian Unity Party.	1985
Oscar Arias Sánchez wins the Nobel Peace Prize for his work creating a regional peace plan for Central America.	1987

World History

1776	The Declaration of Independence is signed.
1789	The French Revolution begins.
1865	The American Civil War ends.
1914	World War I breaks out.
1917	The Bolshevik Revolution brings Communism to Russia.
1929	Worldwide economic depression begins.
1939	World War II begins, following the German invasion of Poland.
1957	The Vietnam War starts.
1989	The Berlin Wall is torn down, as Communism crumbles in Eastern Europe.
1996	Bill Clinton reelected U.S. president.

Fast Facts

Official name: *República de Costa Rica* (Republic of Costa Rica)

Capital: San José

Official language:	Spanish
Official religion:	Roman Catholicism
National anthem:	"*Noble Patria, Tu Hermosa Bandera*" ("Noble Homeland, Your Beautiful Flag")
Government:	Multiparty republic with one legislative house
Chief of state and head of government:	President
Area:	19,730 square miles (51,100 sq km)
Coordinates of geographic center:	10° 0' N, 84° 0' W
Bordering countries:	Costa Rica is bordered on the north by Nicaragua, on the east by the Caribbean Sea, on the southeast by Panama, and on the southwest and west by the Pacific Ocean.
Highest elevation:	Chirripó Grande, 12,530 feet (3,819 m)
Lowest elevation:	Sea level along coasts

Average temperatures (year-round):

Meseta Central	75° to 80°F (24° to 27°C)
Coastlands	100°F (38°C)
Pacific Coast	77° to 100°F (25° to 38°C)

Average annual rainfall:	100 inches (254 cm)
National population (1996):	3,400,000

<table>
<tr><td>Population of
largest cities (1995):</td><td>San José</td><td>321,193</td></tr>
<tr><td></td><td>Metropolitan San José</td><td>959,340</td></tr>
<tr><td></td><td>Limón</td><td>56,525</td></tr>
<tr><td></td><td>Alajuela</td><td>49,115</td></tr>
<tr><td></td><td>San Isidro</td><td>41,513</td></tr>
<tr><td></td><td>Desamparados</td><td>38,858</td></tr>
</table>

Famous landmarks:
- ▶ *Pre-Columbian Gold Museum* (San José)
- ▶ *National Theatre* (San José)
- ▶ *Jade Museum* (San José)

Industry: Agriculture is Costa Rica's main industry. Primary agricultural products include sugarcane, coffee, bananas, and pineapples. Most manufacturing is concentrated in the Meseta Central and major products include food and beverage processing, clothing and shoe production, and electrical appliances.

Currency: Costa Rican colón (¢)=100 céntimos; 1997 exchange rate: $U.S.1=¢214.48.

Weights and measures:	Metric	
Literacy:	94.8%	

Common words and phrases:

¡achará!	What a pity!
bueno	good
buena nota	how cool, great (good note)
¿Cómo está usted?	How are you?
¡diay?	Oh dear, but what can you expect?
gracias	thank you
maje	(used by young men) buddy, pal, or mate
por favor	please
pura vida	great, okay, or cool (pure life)
¿Qué hora es?	What time is it?

Famous Costa Ricans:

Francisco Amíghetti Ruis *Artist*	(1907–)
Oscar Arias Sánchez *President and Nobel Prizewinner*	(1941–)
Fabían Dobles *Writer*	(1918–)
Jose Figueres Ferrer *President*	(1906–1990)
Joaquín García Monge *Writer*	(1907– 1958)

To Find Out More

Nonfiction

▶ Collard, Sneed B. *Monteverde: Science and Scientists in a Costa Rican Cloud Forest*. Danbury, Conn.: Franklin Watts, 1997.

▶ Cummins, Ronnie. *Costa Rica*. Milwaukee: Gareth Stevens, 1990.

▶ Foley, Erin. *Costa Rica*. Tarrytown, N.Y.: Marshall Cavendish, 1997.

▶ Foran, Eileen. *Costa Rica Is My Home*. Milwaukee: Gareth Stevens, 1992.

▶ Patent, Dorothy Hinshaw, and Dan L. Perlan (illustrator). *Children Save the Rain Forest*. New York: Cobblehill, 1996.

▶ Patent, Dorothy Hinshaw, and William Munoz (illustrator). *Biodiversity*. New York: Clarion Books, 1996.

Biography

▶ Gutman, Bill. *Juan Gonzalez: Outstanding Outfielder*. Brookfield, Conn.: Millbrook Press, 1995.

▶ Peduzzi, Kelli. *Oscar Arias: Peacemaker and Leader among Nations*. Milwaukee: Gareth Stevens, 1991.

Fiction

▶ Benavides, Miguel, and Joan Henry (translator). *The Children of Mariplata: Stories from Costa Rica*. Boston: Forest Books, 1992.

▶ Franklin, Kristine L., and Robert Roth (illustrator). *When the Monkeys Came Back*. New York: Atheneum, 1994.

Folktales

▶ Baden, Robert. *And Sunday Makes Seven*. Skokie, Ill.: Albert Whitman, 1990.

Websites

▶ **The Latino Connection**
http://www.ascinsa.com/
LATINOCONNECTION/costari.html
Links to many other sites about
Costa Rica

▶ **The Latin America Network**
http://lanic.utexas.edu/la/ca/cr/
Connections to full texts of Costa
Rica's constitution, the CIA World
Factbook, and many other cultural
and government websites

Organizations and Embassies

▶ **Embassy of Costa Rica**
2114 S Street, N.W.
Washington, DC 20008
(202) 234-2945

▶ **Consulate of Costa Rica**
8 S. Michigan Avenue
Suite 1312
Chicago, IL 60603
(312) 263-2772

Index

Page numbers in *italics* indicate illustrations.

M

N

O

P

Meet the Author

ARION MORRISON graduated from the University of Wales and soon after left for Bolivia to work among Aymara and Quechua people living around Lake Titicaca and in the Andes. In Bolivia, she met her husband, Tony, who was making a series of films about South America for the BBC. Together they have spent the last thirty-five years traveling in Central and South America, Mexico, and Cuba, making television films, writing books, and building up a photographic library specializing in the region. They have two children, now grown up, who have traveled with them many times, in the jungles, mountains, and deserts.

"When writing books, which now number about thirty-five, I find it helps enormously to have visited the countries involved and to have had the opportunity of meeting and talking to the people, as it were, at home. I realize I am very lucky to have been able to do this. It makes a world of difference to spend time with a family, to taste firsthand the country's food, or to experience some of the magnificent sights and scenery.

"Throughout our travels, Tony has been meticulous in keeping detailed notebooks, and it is to these I turn first when beginning a book. Then out comes the map box, and with a large map of the country on the wall in front of me, I begin my serious research for facts and figures. This takes me to my local libraries and others, more specialized, in London. I contact the country's embassy and any other agencies that the country has in the United Kingdom, and of course I surf the web which now provides a wealth of useful material. Finally I make contact with friends and acquaintances who have lived in the country I am writing about. Not only is their knowledge invaluable but they often remind me of things I have forgotten or overlooked."

When not traveling, Ms. Morrison lives in Suffolk, England, with her husband, Tony.

Photo Credits

Photographs ©:

AP/Wide World Photos: 123 (Kent Gilbert); 61, 62, 63

Archive Photos: 57

Art Resource: 49 (Scala)

Brent Winebrenner: 27 top

Corbis-Bettmann: 53, 54 top

Culver Pictures: 54 bottom, 58, 59

D. Donne Bryant Stock Photography: 48, 107 (Tony Alfaro); 79, 103 (Byron Augustin); 44, 113 (Alan Cave); 118 (Sandra W. Earl); 91 (Robert Fried); 90 (Robert F. Kay); 33, 65, 69 top, 76, 78, 101, 132 (Inga Spence); 112, 124

Envision: 126 bottom (Tim Gibson)

Folio, Inc.: 22 (Mark Newman)

Gamma-Liaison: 72 (Kearney), 25, 30

Herb Swanson: 7, 21, 24, 39 bottom, 67, 74, 80 bottom, 81, 83, 84, 89, 93, 95, 96, 110 bottom, 115, 119, 120, 127, 130

International Stock Photo: 88 (Buddy Mays), 16 (Tom Till)

Kevin Schafer: 12, 14, 15, 20, 31, 35 top, 35 bottom, 36, 37, 40, 41, 100, 131

Nik Wheeler: 102, 104

North Wind Picture Archives: 9, 50 top

Photo Researchers: 32 (Gregory Dimijian), 75 (Dan Guravich), 34 (Virginia Weinland)

South American Pictures: 106, 110 top (Jevan Berrange); 5, 27 bottom, 121 (Robert Francis); 69 bottom, 114, 122 (Tony Morrison); 29 (Peter Ryley); 80 top (Chris Sharp)

Stock Montage, Inc.: 55

Superstock, Inc.: 50 bottom

Sygma: 64 (Jason Bleibtreu), 71 (Claude Urraca)

Tony Stone Images: 86, 98 (Tom Benoit); 8 (Gary Braasch); 45, 126 top (Gay Bumgarner); 26 (Jacques Jangoux); 17 (Hilarie Kavanagh); 105, 116 (Martin Rogers); spine, 39 top, 42, (Kevin Schafer); 38 (Tom Ulrich); cover, back cover, 6 (Denis Waugh)

Victor Englebert: 18, 23

Maps by Joe LeMonnier